I0621139

SHED BOY

A Hidden Creek Mystery

Cheryl K. Smith

karmadillo Press   *   Cheshire OR

karmadillo Press
22705 Hwy 36
Cheshire OR 97419
USA
541 505-6440
www.karmadillo.com

Author: Cheryl K. Smith
Cover Design: Zodiakk Books

This is a work of fiction.
Any similarities to people or places, living or dead, is purely coincidental.

Printed and bound in the United States of America

Chapter 1

Pearl Kelly's picture-perfect life had hit a bump. Her shed boy was missing.

She sat on the front porch with her little white Pomeranian, Buckley, twirling one of her dark curls. She was deep in thought and oblivious to the fat red-breasted robins searching for food in her front yard. *Where had Pat gone?* The van was still parked by the barn, so if he went somewhere, it was on foot. She felt cross. She had already registered her goats for the goat show, which was in 10 days, and she counted on him to help.

They were supposed to start clipping the goats today for a show, so they would have a little grow-out and not be totally pink-skinned and bald. They always look better after their coats have grown a few weeks, according to her friends in the goat club, so she should have gotten started a week ago. She had 10 goats, but Pearl had registered just the two adult does and two dry yearlings for her first show.

Pearl looked out over her property, Hidden Creek Farm, thinking about how lucky she was to have found it two years ago. It was five acres in an unincorporated area in the Oregon Coast Range called Middle Pass. It had several fenced pastures and a year-round creek that ran through it. The property was bordered on two sides by old growth fir trees, vine maples, and flowering dogwood. Sitting atop a gentle sloping hill, she could view most of the property and across the highway to a forested hill.

It was perfect for her, with a cute house, a barn, a chicken coop, and different pastures for the goats and whatever other livestock she decided to raise. She was far enough off the highway that the intermittent traffic noises were muffled, yet she could see when someone approached on her long driveway. And Buckley had the freedom to run free—a far cry from his life in the city, where he had been either indoors or on a leash.

Pearl finished her coffee and returned to the kitchen, where she put the empty coffee cup into the sink. She walked into the bedroom, where she took off her ratty bathrobe, flung it onto a chair, and grabbed the clean cotton socks she had left on the same chair earlier. She glanced at her pudgy figure in the mirror and sighed as she slipped the socks onto her feet and stepped back into her fuzzy slippers. She moved to the mud room, where she put on moss green, short-sleeved coveralls over her nightgown and stepped out of her slippers and into her muck boots. Buckley knew the daily drill; he had already moved into his dog bed for a morning nap.

She put the stainless-steel milk pail and strainer and half-gallon glass mason jar into a blue plastic tote—along with a red plastic pail and a rag for washing udders—and started for the barn. On the way, she detoured to the shed under the white dogwood and knocked on the door. No answer. She opened it a crack and called out, "Pat." She could see that he wasn't in the bed. Just as Pearl thought, Pat hadn't come home last night. She felt uneasy; this wasn't like him.

She would have to put it out of her mind for now; chores needed to be done no matter what. Pearl made her way to the barn with the milking equipment. She went in through the side door to the milk room, where she laid out the equipment and began her chores.

She slid open the big side barn door wider, then added hay to the hay racks and greeted the goats as she entered. She studied each goat, one at a time; she had read in one of her goat books that it was the most important first step for keeping your goats healthy. They all seemed to be acting in character—the pushy ones pushed and the quiet ones avoided the pushy ones. The kids let out loud cries from the stall where they had been isolated from their mothers the night before so Pearl could take the milk. She threw them some hay to hold them over for another 20 minutes or so while she milked their dams. She stuffed two flakes of hay into the bucks' hay feeder on the other side of the barn.

Pearl washed and dried her hands at the sink. She filled the red bucket with warm soapy water and carried it to the milk room, where she placed it next to her other milking equipment. One at a time, she let the two adult does into the milk room, where they jumped on the stand to eat their grain while she washed and dried their udders and milked them. After she filtered the milk into clean jars and put them in the barn fridge to cool, Pearl freed the kids—

who rushed to their mothers and attempted to nurse. She emptied and refilled the water buckets and headed for the chicken coop to let the hens into the run, throw out some scratch, and refill their water. She would let them out to free range later in the day.

Her stomach growled, a sensation that let her know it was time for her second cup of coffee and some breakfast. Most mornings, Cheerios would do, but today she craved something special and needed to use some of the eggs that had accumulated. She made oatmeal pancakes and topped them with whipped cream and blackberries she had harvested from the bushes along the driveway that led to the house. She savored each bite, while she reviewed the rules and timelines for the upcoming goat show. She had so much to do to get her goats ready for their first show!

After she cleaned the milking equipment and finished washing breakfast dishes, Pearl would walk over to her neighbor Jane Wilson's house, where she suspected she would find Pat. She shook her head in annoyance; *he knew they had a lot to do to get ready for the fair, so why hadn't he come home this morning?*

She put on a flower print blouse, blue leggings, and Crocs, then clipped her hair up. She and Buckley exited out the back door and down to the path in the woods that connected their back yards. She jumped over the narrowest part of the creek. By the end of summer, the creek had slowed to little more than a mucky trickle in most spots. Buckley wasn't keen on jumping; being a dog, he instead chose to walk through the slow-flowing water. He stirred up the mud as he slogged through. Pearl dreaded Jane's reaction when she saw a muddy dog. As far as Pearl could tell, Jane wasn't an animal lover. All of her passion seemed directed toward plants.

Jane was a master gardener and had a beautiful property. *Why can't I have a green thumb,* thought Pearl. In two years' time, Pearl had managed to destroy most of the landscaping the prior owners had meticulously cared for. Now invasive Himalayan blackberries, Queen Anne's lace, prickly thistles, and purple-flowered knapweed had begun to dominate the area between the creek and driveway. Aesthetics were not her thing; she was all about practicality.

They entered Jane's back garden through a magnificent arch enveloped in wisteria. The garden featured potted plants, hanging plants, trees, bushes, shrubs, and an explosion of flowers—echinacea, bee balm, petunias, roses, and many others she couldn't identify. God and goddess statues were placed throughout.

The side yards were dedicated to exotic plants from different locales, each labeled with a little metal sign—Anthurium, Cerbera odallam, Cotinus coggygria, Bird of Paradise, Lily of the Valley, Japanese maple, and more. Last month Jane had entered the Middle Pass Garden Club's annual Best Garden Contest and Tour and, of course, she had taken grand prize for the third time. Her garden had been featured more than once in the *Middle Pass Gazette* and the electric co-op's magazine.

Buckley and Pearl wound their way through the garden path to the house's back door and up the three cement steps. Pearl gingerly wrung out some of the water from his once fluffy coat and tried to wipe the little dog's mucky paws on the rug in front of the door, but found it futile. She picked him up and held him out a little from her body to avoid getting muddy herself. She didn't think Jane would want him on her floor—but if she left him outside, who knew where he might dig. She held Buckley with both hands and struggled to pull open the wooden screen door with a free finger. She kicked at the bottom of the inner door in lieu of knocking.

Jane, a thin woman with rat brown hair in two thick braids, frowned as she opened the back door and saw Pearl standing there with the bedraggled, formerly white dog. Pearl pasted on a fake smile and pushed her way through the door into the entryway, which contained a sink, washer and dryer, and shelves that overflowed with garden equipment, gloves, seed packets, potting soil, and fertilizer.

"Don't worry, I'll hold my dog," Pearl said defensively. "Do you have a towel I can use to wipe his feet and wrap him in?" She continued to hold him away from her body, in an attempt to keep the mud off her blouse.

"I suppose," said Jane in an irritated voice. "Why are you here?"

Pearl and Jane had both made efforts to develop a friendship when Pearl first moved to the area, but Jane's neediness conflicted with Pearl's perceived independent streak.

Jane's husband had died suddenly after being hit by the letter carrier in a freak accident three years before Pearl moved to the area. Jane had been trying to fill the hole in her life ever since. She and her husband had owned a garden store together, as well as both being avid gardeners. According to what Pearl had heard, they had spent most every moment of their 20-year marriage together and liked it that way.

Pearl had little in common with Jane and could only take so much of the woman. They even communicated differently; while Pearl was inclined to get right to the point, Jane often got carried away with her stories, veering off the subject repeatedly. Shortly after they met, Jane had started coming over to visit on a daily basis, until Pearl told her that she preferred not to spend so much time with other people. She could do just fine without a partner or a neighbor to get in her way. To Pearl's way of thinking, Jane had overreacted. She had not visited Pearl's house more than twice since that conversation.

"I was just being sociable, and I wanted to congratulate you on your Garden Club win. Your garden is absolutely beautiful. You have quite the green thumb," Pearl said as they moved toward the dining room table in the kitchen area. Jane left and returned with a tattered brown towel from the bathroom. She handed it to Pearl.

The kitchen was as cluttered as the back room, with succulents in the window and other plants on countertops, competing for space with dishes and cooking paraphernalia. The sun shone in the window over the sink, so it provided an ideal spot for indoor plants. On the wall above the table were two shadow boxes, one with various dried herbs and another with beautiful but dead butterflies. The round dining room table was obscured by a fruit-patterned oilcloth table covering, and the half of the table nearest the wall was buried under a Kleenex box, an empty shadow box, a bowl with some large seeds in it, a few garden magazines, knickknacks, and a small spray bottle used to mist plants. The rest of the table was empty except for one half-filled coffee cup and a plate with crumbs on it. *Unless he had stayed over and was still asleep, Pat wasn't there.*

Pearl took the proffered towel and placed it and then Buckley on her lap. She wiped her hands and wrapped the sides of the towel around him.

"Would you like coffee or tea?" asked Jane, as she wiped her hand on leggings. *If nothing else, she had good manners.*

"Tea," said Pearl, stroking Buckley. "Do you have any mint tea?"

"Of course, I do. What kind do you want? I have spearmint, chocolate mint, ginger mint, lemon mint...." The slender woman put out one finger as she named each type, as though counting.

"Just plain peppermint," Pearl snapped, a little too harshly. "I am not much of a connoisseur when it comes to tea. You are so much more knowledgeable about herbs than I am." She smiled, hoping to take the sting out of her abruptness with the compliment.

Once they each had a cup of piping hot herbal tea, they launched into small talk, discussing the Garden Club Tour, Pearl's plans for the fair, and the weather. After they had run out of things to talk about, Pearl proceeded to what she had come for. "Have you seen Pat today?"

"Why would I see Pat?" Jane frowned and crossed her arms.

"Oh, I thought you two were seeing each other." Pearl laughed nervously. *Jane was so desperate she would settle for anyone.* Pat wasn't Pearl's type, if anyone was. Although he could be charming and witty, that big beer gut and waddling walk were a turnoff for her. Not that she was in the market, anyway. Pat had half-heartedly flirted with her a few times in the early days, but he soon got the message that she wasn't interested.

"No, we aren't!" Jane retorted.

"Oh, sorry...." said Pearl, taken aback. "It's just that I haven't seen him since yesterday, the van is still at the farm, and he is nowhere to be found. I'm worried about him." She took the last gulp of tea, savoring the mint flavor.

Pearl thought it best to drop the subject, even though she didn't believe Jane. She had gotten the answer to her question. Jane hadn't seen Pat that day. After an awkward silence and no eye contact from Jane, Pearl's frustration was telegraphed to Buckley, who began to squirm in her lap.

Pearl looked at him and then back at Jane, and put both palms out and raised her eyebrows in feigned exasperation. She was glad for the excuse to leave. The creases between Jane's eyes deepened and she frowned at Pearl. She sat rigid.

"I think Buckley is done with visiting. I'm sorry to have to run off so soon. I have so much to do to get ready for the goat show. Thank you for the tea! We must get together like this more often," Pearl said insincerely as she stood and headed for the back door. "No need to get up. I can let myself out."

There was still no sign of Pat when they got back to the farm. Pearl knocked on the shed door but got no answer. She opened the door a crack and peered in. Nothing but the odor of unwashed clothing and bedding. She didn't want to invade his privacy, but she needed to check to make sure he hadn't returned to take a nap while she was away.

While she figured out what to do next, she would take the goats for a walk. She took the does, and sometimes the bucks, out in the woods on most days the weather permitted, so they could get their exercise and eat the browse that is the mainstay of a goat's diet. The hikes were relaxing for her and she did her best thinking out in the woods.

On the porch, Pearl put overalls on over her clothes and switched her crocs for muck boots. She and Buckley trotted out to the barn, where she got a large, blue plastic bowl and put a handful of grain in the bottom. She needed to lure the goats to the woods and away from the shrubbery and few other plants around her house that were still alive. They would like nothing better than to eat her lilac bush! She opened the gate, rattled the grain bowl, and the goats rushed from the barn toward her. She trotted in the direction of the woods with the herd of does and kids hot on her heels. Once they were a few feet along the path, she set the bowl on the ground, and they crowded around it. The little ones squeezed in to try to get their share of what seemed so appealing. In only minutes the goats had finished the grain and turned their attention to the vegetation along the path.

Buckley knew the routine and didn't want to get stepped on, so he ran ahead on the path. Pearl followed him. Behind her the goats, as is their way, took nibbles here and there and eventually moved on. The herd ambled down the path for 10 or 15 minutes until they arrived at the big log that had fallen over the creek. She looked up to see Buckley already standing in the middle of the log. Pearl climbed up to join him, with arms out to maintain her balance as she crossed. The goats jumped up and followed. A line of them trotted across the decaying log and intermittently stopped to eat what little vegetation grew from it. The little tri-color buckling tried to jump up, fell, and began to scream for his mother. On the second try, he succeeded and ran across the log, where he almost knocked another kid off into the trickle of a stream.

Once they got to the other side, the goats took the lead and continued the hike with countless stops and starts, until they reached a huge stand of blackberry bushes near a fork in the trail. Ahead was a fork in the path that led to the main road into Middle Pass. They began to gobble leaves and the few remaining berries—goat candy. As Pearl and Buckley caught up with them, a rabbit farther along the path took off running. That was Buckley's signal to accelerate and sprint in the same direction. Pearl had been about to yell at him to quit chasing wildlife when he abruptly stopped. She looked farther up the path and saw legs and feet at the curve where Buckley stood.

She strode toward the dog, her heart pounding. As Pearl approached, she saw a body, lying face-down, with the head partially covered by blackberry vines. Farther along, she spied a black flashlight with a dim beam about a foot beyond the body. She immediately recognized the red plaid shirt. Pat! She ran to him and put her fingers around his wrist to check for a pulse. Nothing. In fact, his body had already stiffened from rigor mortis. She noticed a small pool of vomit nearby. She shuddered and looked around. *Who could have done this to him?* No one was in sight.

Pearl whirled around and yelled at Buckley to come. The goats sensed her panic and began to race along the trail then up and over the log toward home. As prey animals, panic drove them back to their safe place in the barn. Pearl grabbed Buckley and carried him down the trail and across the log after the goats, walking as fast as she could.

Chapter 2

The sheriff arrived at Pearl's house about 20 minutes after her frantic call. In normal circumstances, law enforcement took their time to get out to Middle Pass. In many cases, they didn't bother to drive out at all; they just sent paperwork for crime victims to fill out. Pearl was relieved to learn that they could respond quickly when needed.

By the time the sheriff got there, three male first responders from the volunteer fire department—one who drove the ambulance—were already milling around in her yard, chattering and making jokes. They were all local men of different ages, wearing plaid flannel shirts or hoodies and jeans. Buckley was in the house with Pearl, yapping his little head off. She had answered the door when one of the men—an out-of-shape, balding fellow with a beer gut hanging over his jeans—knocked on the door. Pearl informed them that she would wait inside for the sheriff and they were welcome to sit on the porch.

Pearl didn't tell the first responders where Pat's body was located because she had watched enough true crime to know that you don't want people to contaminate a potential crime scene. Although she knew Pat may have had an accident, something didn't feel right. That pool of vomit. She had known him for more than two years now and, unlike her, he didn't have a sensitive stomach. He also wasn't a drinker.

Pearl saw Sheriff Dan Springer maneuver into the driveway behind the other vehicles and get out of his car. He was a tall, wiry man, handsome in a rugged way in his tan uniform, with a lined face and a shock of gray hair. He spoke briefly to the men in her front yard and then walked toward the porch, where Pearl met him as she slid out the door, using her foot to keep Buckley inside.

"How are you, Pearl? It sounds like you had quite a shock. You called about a body?" said the sheriff. He squinted against the sun. "I'm surprised to see you here. For some reason I thought you lived in town. Tell me about the body you found."

She nodded somberly. "My shed—I mean my handyman, Pat. Out in the woods. I was taking the goats on a walk and my dog found him on the path. I think it was about 11:45 this morning when we found him. The body is already in rigor mortis. I can show you where the path starts on Crown Road. It's easier to get there in a vehicle, and it will also be easier to transport his body out of there, too. If you take the path behind my house, you have to walk across a log over the creek."

"You didn't touch anything, did you?" Sheriff Springer asked, holding his hand above his eyes to block the sun's glare.

"No, other than checking his pulse. Remember, I'm a nurse, Dan. Er, retired nurse," Pearl corrected herself. She chewed on her lip, a nervous habit she had had since

14

childhood. "I purposely didn't tell the first responders where the body is because I didn't want them to contaminate the scene."

"Of course; I'm not suggesting you didn't know what you were doing. You were always a good nurse," he replied. "I just have to ask these questions. Why don't you get in my car and we'll go check it out."

She walked toward his car and stood by the passenger side while he stopped and again spoke to the men who had arrived earlier. He continued to the big black car and climbed into the driver's seat, signaling for Pearl to get in.

Pearl didn't bother to lock the house. No one in these parts did. Besides, she had read that people who wanted to break into a house prefer those without dogs barking inside. She could hear Buckley yipping as she walked across the front yard. Pearl even kept the keys in her farm van so Pat could use it to buy feed without having to bother her. She opened the door and slid into the passenger seat.

They rolled down her driveway and turned right onto the highway, while the men in her yard clambered back into their vehicles and followed them. No need to rush at this point.

They took a right onto Crown Road toward the village of Middle Pass. They had driven less than half a mile when Pearl said "Pull over here." The hiking path began between two tall fir trees on the right.

They climbed out of the car as the ambulance and another car pulled up. Pearl led the way and Sheriff Springer followed her along the path, which crossed the

15

timber reserve behind Jane's property. As they approached the blackberry bushes near where Pearl and the goats had been walking when she found the body, she slowed her pace. With the sheriff on her heels, she reached the other path and glanced to her right. There lay Pat's body, his head mostly covered by blackberry vines.

"Here he is," she said, pointing. She felt a pang of loss.

"Okay," murmured the sheriff. "You need to go back and wait in the car. It shouldn't take me too long." He started toward the body.

The first responders caught up with them. The sheriff turned around and held up a hand. "Stand back for now. We don't want to do anything to interfere, in case it's a crime scene."

He extracted latex gloves from his pocket and put them on, then knelt by Pat's body and turned it over. He put his fingers on the carotid artery to confirm that Pat was deceased.

"Pearl was right. It appears that he's been deceased for a while."

He checked his watch for the time, pulled out a tan notebook and pen, and began to take notes. Pearl turned and headed back to Crown Road. A wave of sadness washed over her as she traipsed back to the police car; after all, Pat, despite his faults, had been a friend.

As she waited in the car for the sheriff, she saw another police car arrive. A man in a suit and a woman in uniform got out and walked into the woods on the path, stopping to talk briefly to two first responders who were on their way back out. She watched the men get a stretcher from the ambulance and carry it into the woods. About 20 minutes had gone by when the sheriff emerged from the path. He walked around to the driver's side of the patrol car and got in.

"It appears to be an accident, but we'll have to see what the medical examiner thinks." He rubbed his chin. "It looks like he fell and hit his head on a stump that the blackberry bushes had grown over. That's all that is obvious right now."

Pearl closed her eyes and shook her head in disbelief. She didn't believe it was an accident. Pat knew that trail. And why was his body facing south, like he was heading toward town? Someone must have followed him and hit him.

The sheriff started the car and drove back toward Pearl's house.

"How long have you lived out here?" asked the sheriff. "I didn't realize you lived so far from the hospital."

"I moved here a few years ago. I had always dreamed of having dairy goats, so when I retired, I spent the next year searching for the perfect place. I found it here. I figured I would start with chickens and a small garden and then get goats. I planned to sell eggs, milk, and cheese. I haven't gotten into making cheese for sale yet."

"I guess I'm behind on the news. I wasn't aware you were no longer working at the hospital." The sheriff's eyes lit up. "So you sell milk? We had a few goats when I was growing up and I was raised on goat milk."

17

Pearl laughed in delight, "Yes. It's $8 a half gallon, and you need to supply your own jars. I can give the first one to you for a $1.50 deposit. Nigerian Dwarf goat milk has high butterfat and is some of the sweetest. It's much better than cow milk, as you probably know. They don't give as much milk as full-sized goats, but they are so colorful and easy to handle." She loved to talk about goats.

They pulled into her driveway and he stopped the car. "I'd like to come by and get some milk later. I'm not off work for a couple hours and don't want it to get warm. But I need to ask you some questions about Pat, if you have the time now."

"Sure," said Pearl. "Are you hungry? With all this excitement I completely forgot to eat lunch. I was going to have some tea and a sandwich."

"I had lunch already, but you know what I would really like? A glass of your cold goat milk." His eyes twinkled.

"Done," she said. "If you don't mind me eating in front of you. Just give me a minute to put on the kettle and make a cheese sandwich. And, just to warn you, my dog Buckley won't like you at first. Not that he bites or anything. Just sit down at the dining room table when you get in the house and let him come to you."

They got out of the car and walked toward the porch. Buckley could be heard barking inside. Pearl opened the door and led the way in, while Buckley increased his barking and backed toward the couch.

Sheriff Springer pulled out a dining room chair and plopped down at the table. He pretended Buckley wasn't there. "Can he have a biscuit?" he asked with a smile. Pearl nodded.

A dog lover, he always carried some small biscuits in his pocket, so he placed one on the floor near his feet while Pearl turned on a burner and filled the tea kettle. She opened the fridge and pulled out a glass bottle of milk, a jar of mayonnaise, and a package of cheddar cheese. She filled a glass with the milk and set it on the table in front of the sheriff. She cut two slices of seeded wheat bread from the loaf on the cutting board and made a sandwich. By then the kettle had begun to whistle, so she poured the boiling water over a black tea bag and carried the cup and her sandwich to the table.

By this time Buckley was already on his second biscuit and had begun to paw at the sheriff's leg.

"He doesn't usually like men, so I'm surprised he came around so quickly, even with the biscuits," she said between bites.

The sheriff laughed. "I guess I just got lucky." He took a big drink of milk. "This is as good as you said. It's been years since I had any."

"So many people have the idea that goat milk tastes bad, despite never tasting it. I've tried milk from different breeds and I think the Nigerian Dwarf milk is some of the best." Pearl said proudly.

Once she had finished her sandwich, the sheriff pulled out his notepad and began the questions.

"What is Pat's full name?"

"Patrick Steinberg. I don't know if he has a middle name."

"How did you know him?"

"He was my 'shed boy.' That is, he helped me around the farm and in exchange I let him live in the 10 x 12 shed I had here, fed him the occasional meal, and paid him a small stipend. He wasn't necessarily the hardest or most reliable worker, but he was a help."

"Do you know his age or birthdate?"

"He was born October 8, 1964. He would have been 58 next month." Pearl teared up as she spoke.

"How did you meet him?"

"When I lived in town, I used to volunteer at the annual Christmas dinner in Eugene for unhoused people. About five years ago, we had started talking. I found him well-read and funny, if not a little abrasive and defensive. He tended to rub people the wrong way. He had a habit of arguing even when the other person agreed with him. But there was something likeable about him. Over the years, I learned, mostly, to walk away when he got angry and acted crazy.

"After that dinner, I bumped into Pat again at a coffee shop where I sometimes hung out, which led to a friendship of sorts. He seemed lonely and harmless. I started meeting him for coffee regularly and took him out for a dinner a few times and I helped him get on the SNAP food program. I wasn't sure exactly where he lived, although he talked about the library and university as good places to sleep or hang out. I seemed to run into him at the coffee shop frequently.

"Months after I got my goats, I realized I could use some help. I cautiously decided to offer him a job and the extra bedroom in my house. I don't know what I was thinking. I figured it would help him, too. Of course, he would have to continue to stay sober and could only smoke outside, as well as follow any other rules I had.

"Well, it took less than a month to regret my decision—not that he wasn't helping around the farm; I just couldn't have him living in my home. He was getting the wrong idea about his role. I had the extra shed, which was wired for electric but wasn't being used much, got one of those oil-filled electric heaters, rented a port-a-potty, and offered it to him.

"Pat wasn't thrilled about being 'booted out of the house,' as he referred to it. I explained to him as gently as possible that I needed my privacy, so he could either go back to town or make do with what I was offering. I had to give him a wide berth while he stomped around the farm, muttering under his breath about how women think they're in charge, but he finally acquiesced—while continuing to complain about it to anyone who would listen."

The sheriff let out a guffaw. "Sounds like an interesting situation. So you had about a year to work things out? How was it going?"

"He adapted to the situation, and with a roof over his head and some money in his pocket, his behavior seemed to improve. He acted less erratic and even developed some friendships in the area. Occasionally a friend he had known in town would come out to visit, in fact he introduced me to that friend, who helped out here a few times when the job was beyond Pat's skill level. He even had a few short-lived romantic relationships."

"When did you last see him?" The sheriff looked down in surprise at the little white puffball in his lap and chuckled. They had been so busy talking that neither of them had noticed when Buckley jumped up.

"I saw him yesterday morning. He cleaned a stall for me and we talked about getting ready for the goat show where I plan to show my goats for the first time. We didn't have any definite plans for yesterday, so I thought nothing of not seeing him. He frequently walks or takes the van to town, and I think he eats at the café fairly often."

The sheriff made a note on his pad. "Were you home yesterday afternoon and evening?"

Pearl pondered the question for a minute, biting her lower lip. "In the afternoon, yes. I attended a goat club meeting from 6:00 to 9:00 or so in the evening."

"So you didn't see him last night?" The sheriff scratched Buckley behind the ears.

"No, and I didn't hear anything after I got home either. I usually know when he comes or goes on the path behind the house because Buckley always alerts me with his barking." Pearl smiled at the dog on the sheriff's lap. "I had started to think that Pat was in a relationship with my neighbor, Jane, because Buckley would bark when Pat went that way at night on the path behind our properties. But today when I went over there looking for him, she got mad and denied it. You might want to ask her if she's seen him. Maybe you'll get a different answer than I did."

The sheriff raised his eyebrows. "Do you know how I can get ahold of any of his other friends?"

"No, I don't have phone numbers or anything. He doesn't have a cell phone, either."

"Can you think of any reason anyone would want to hurt him?"

Pearl thought for a minute. "Well, like I said, he did have a tendency to be rude and argumentative. But while lots of people found him annoying, I can't imagine it would have been enough to kill him over. But now that I think about it, he did just inherit some money from a distant uncle who died. I don't know how much it was or if he had gotten the money yet; he was pretty secretive with me."

"Does he drink or use drugs?"

"Well, yes, he does smoke pot, like a lot of people around here. But he quit drinking probably three years ago. One requirement when he moved here was that he not drink. He had gotten into trouble with alcohol in the past. Nothing criminal or anything—he just got more obnoxious than usual."

"Any idea why he would have been on that path at night?"

"Not really. It seemed odd to me that he would have been heading in the direction of town. Especially at night. I'm still puzzling that one out." Pearl sighed.

The sheriff closed his notebook and put it back in his pocket. "I think that's all I need from you for now. I'll be back with an empty jar to buy some milk in the next day or two. We'll have to wait for the medical examiner to determine the cause of death. I didn't see any footprints in the area; the soil is so dry this time of year, that we wouldn't be able to see anything unless there was a scuffle. I think it was just a freak accident."

Pearl furrowed her brow. "There was just one more thing. Did you notice that he had vomited? I thought it was unusual because although he didn't believe in doctors, he never seemed to get sick. The last time I saw him, he had seemed fine. And it also seems unlikely that he would have accidentally fallen in a way that his head was mostly covered by the blackberry vines."

"I did see the vomit, and we collected it for evidence just in case. Still, to my eye, it looks like he fell, hitting his head on the stump under the blackberries. I did notice that he had some puncture wounds from the thorns on his face and neck. Those could have occurred during a fall. Once I learn more from the medical examiner, I'll let you know for sure.

"Are you around most of the time or should I call before I come over to buy milk?"

"Just stop by. I'm usually here. I would appreciate being in the loop for your investigation. I have a feeling that this was no accident." Pearl looked hopeful.

"No problem." The sheriff set Buckley on the floor and let himself out.

Chapter 3

Pearl lay in bed that morning until 7:30, her mind racing. She felt tired after tossing and turning all night, but hyperactive at the same time. She would go into Pat's shed this morning after chores and hunt for clues. She had no idea what she might be looking for, other than more details about the inheritance that he had mentioned. He was so secretive about anything having to do with money.

But she had more immediate concerns. She had to start clipping her show goats and figure out how she would be able to get everything she needed to the goat show by herself.

Buckley noticed her stirring and jumped off the bed, rolled around on the floor, and jumped back up. He walked across the blanket to her face protruding from the covers, with his tail wagging, and licked her twice before she could stop him. "Buckley! No face licking," she said, unable to stop herself from laughing. The little guy always brightened her life.

Pearl threw back the covers and rolled out of bed. She stepped into her slippers and took her bathrobe from the chair where she had thrown it and slipped into it. She sauntered down the hall to the kitchen and opened the door to let Buckley out. She left the door unlatched so he could knock it open when he wanted to come back in. Then she walked into the pantry, scooped out some kibble, and padded to his bowl, where she dumped the food.

Now she could attend to her needs. Pearl ground two scoops of coffee beans in her little electric grinder, dumped them into a filter that lined the top of the pot, filled water to the four-cup line, and flicked the switch on. Once it had stopped dripping and Buckley had finished his breakfast, she poured a cup, added some goat milk, and they moved to the porch. The weather was cool in the mornings, but still nice. The clouds would burn off in a few hours for a pleasant day.

Pearl drank her coffee while she skimmed the online *New York Times*. She found the Spelling Bee and Wordle— two of her favorite games—and completed them. Since she had retired, she made an effort to keep her brain active. She believed these games, along with crosswords, would help. Once she finished the newspaper, she sat back, petted Buckley, and resumed her ruminations about Pat's death.

She finished her coffee and shook her head to stop the obsessive thinking. She couldn't dilly-dally any longer; it was time for the morning chores. She took her iPad and empty cup into the house and prepared her milking equipment.

As she did the morning chores, she noticed that the does and their babies seemed calmer than usual. She figured they must be getting used to the kids being locked up at night. That didn't stop the little rascals from racing madly for their empty-uddered mothers once she let them loose, though. Pearl was famished after she finished the chores and had to eat before she took on the clipping.

After her breakfast, Pearl ambled out to Pat's shed/house. She would have to clean it out anyway and figure out what to do with his meager belongings. With Buckley at her heels, she scanned the area, then cautiously opened the door. She couldn't help but feel that she was intruding in some way. She had always respected Pat's privacy in the past and was having a hard time coming to terms with the idea of him being dead.

A twin mattress lay on the floor next to one wall, with a blanket and sheets crumpled on it, and pillow with a dirty pillowcase near the top. Next to it an apple crate rested on its side, with some books stacked in the bottom and a small lamp on top. A chair sat in the corner, piled with clothing and next to a small nightstand with two drawers. On the far wall a small fold-out table held a dust-covered microwave. The rest of the table was buried in a variety of clutter—a stack of folded paper bags, opened and unopened mail, magazines, paperback books, empty soda cans, a partial loaf of bread, and to-go containers from the café. Under the table sat a dorm-sized refrigerator, which contained some sodas, lunch meat, condiments, and cheese. The microwave, refrigerator, heater, and lamp were plugged into a surge protector, which was attached to the only electric outlet in the shed.

Pearl rummaged through the mail on the table until she discovered a thick envelope with an attorney's office return address in Portland. She opened it and read through the documents, learning that Pat had been left $5,000, which would be sent once the estate closed. It was dated six months previous. She also found another envelope with a letter from the prior week that referenced an attached check—which was nowhere to be seen. She rifled through the cluttered nightstand drawers where she found $175 in various bills and a jar half-filled with coins mixed with a variety of junk. Pearl added the bills to the jar of cash and took it for safekeeping.

So he had gotten his inheritance! Pearl wondered whether it was part of the personal property that the sheriff collected at the scene. She would have to ask him when he came back. If Pat didn't have the check or money on him when he died, the sheriff would have to agree that it looked suspicious.

She left everything else as she had found it, closed the door, and walked back toward the house. As she neared the front porch a vehicle crept up the driveway. She turned in that direction and saw that it was a dark blue van. *Who could it be?* Buckley began to bark at the vehicle, but stuck close to Pearl. As it pulled closer, Pearl recognized the driver: Westin Denton.

"Good morning, Westin! What are you doing here?" Pearl was thrilled. Buckley jumped at his legs, tail going like crazy. He remembered Westin from the other times he had been to the farm to help out.

What perfect timing.

Pearl had met Westin through Pat, who knew him from the streets in town. In his 30s, Westin was about 25 years younger than Pat, stronger, and with a lot more skills.

He had helped Pearl with building, fencing, and troubleshooting problems around the farm. Her spirits soared. Maybe he would be the solution to her challenge of getting all the goats to the show. What a strange coincidence that he would show up today.

Westin often came around when he needed money. He knew that with a farm, she always required help with something. He had proven to be trustworthy over the past year and he, like Pat, was self-educated so Pearl enjoyed having him around and talking to him. On top of that, Buckley had decided Westin was his best friend.

Westin bent over and picked up the wriggling Pomeranian and held him under his arm while they talked. "I drove to the coast last week during that weird heat wave. I just got back. I decided to stop and say hello and see if you had any projects for me to work on."

"Actually, I do. I don't suppose you heard about what happened to Pat."

"No; what happened to him? Is he here?" Buckley began to squirm, so Westin put him on the ground.

"Buckley found his body on the path that leads to Crown Road yesterday around noon when we were on a hike with the goats." Pearl bit her lip and a tear trickled down her cheek. "I don't know where he was going but they're saying it was an accident," she said, her voice cracking.

"What? What kind of accident?" Westin's eyes widened and he put his hand on Pearl's arm to steady her.

"He was lying on the ground with his head in a stand of blackberry bushes. The sheriff thinks he fell and hit his head on a stump that was under them. I think it's unlikely that he would have landed like that and hit his head hard enough to kill him if it was a simple fall." Pearl started crying.

"That's terrible! I know sometimes we didn't get along, but I considered him a good friend," said Westin. He shook his head in disbelief, released her arm, and studied the ground.

Pearl wiped her eyes and took a deep breath, gathering her emotions. "Something seems off to me. He was headed away from the house and he had thrown up. He had his flashlight with him, too. I'm sure he wasn't sick, though. At least he wasn't that morning when he was mucking the stalls in the barn. Anyway, the sheriff is going to get back to me once the medical examiner makes a definitive finding on the cause of death."

"Wow. That's crazy," said Westin, still shaking his head. "Is there anything I can do?"

"Not about his death, but he was supposed to help me with the goats I entered in the goat show at the fairgrounds, and now everything is going to fall on me. I can get them ready, but I need help to get them loaded. I had started to depend on him so much."

Westin turned to survey the farm. "When do you have to go?"

"In less than two weeks. Will you be around?" she gazed at him intently. Buckley had wandered off and started eating grass.

"I can be. We can talk about the specifics when it gets closer. Is there anything you need right now?"

"Oh, my goodness! That would be so great if you could. I can handle all the goat preparation myself even though I hadn't planned on it. Do you need some money right now?" Pearl would find something for him to do, if necessary, so he didn't commit himself to a project somewhere else. "I'm sure I have some work you could do if you need it now."

"No, I had planned to go in and see my friends in Eugene tonight. I'll call you or come by so we can stay in touch." He crouched and patted the ground to call Buckley over, then playfully grabbed him. They tussled for a few minutes. Pearl grinned.

"I'm glad I stopped by. I'll see you later." He walked over and gave her a big hug. He is such a nice young man, thought Pearl as she hugged back.

"Oh, and one more thing," said Pearl. "Do you know if Pat had any family?"

"Not that I know of. Why?" Westin backed toward his van.

"Oh, nothing really. I just need to figure out who, if anyone, to give his stuff to."

Pearl, her dark curls pulled into a messy ponytail, sat at the dining room table re-reading the goat show rules and the chapter of *Raising Goats for Dummies* on showing. She imagined herself winning ribbons for each category her goats were in. She had been practicing with the older does for several months now. If she could win Best of Breed and Best Udder, along with some first-place ribbons, she would be ecstatic.

Buckley's sudden barking jolted her from her fantasy. A moment later someone knocked at the front door. *What now?* She flipped on the front porch light, held a yapping Buckley back with her right foot, and pulled the door open a crack. There stood a handsome, middle-aged man dressed in a grey hoody and jeans. For a second she didn't recognize Sheriff Dan Springer without the uniform. He held an empty, clean half-gallon jar.

"Sorry to come by so late, but I wanted to get back to you regarding what we found out about Pat. And I figured it would be a good time to finally get some of your delicious milk," said the sheriff with a grin. He bent over to pet Buckley, which was all it took to quiet him.

"Come in, Dan. Have a seat. Can I offer you something to drink?"

He held up a hand, "No, no thanks. I don't want to take too much of your time." He pulled out a dining room chair and sat. Buckley retreated to his dog bed next to the woodstove.

Pearl pushed aside the show booklet and turned her attention to the sheriff. "What did you find out?" She bit her lip nervously.

"It appears that Pat may have died around 8:30 or 9 pm. His blood alcohol was a .06. So he had been drinking, which could have made it more likely that he was unsteady enough to fall. The medical examiner has provisionally ruled it an accident. I think Pat just got unlucky and hit that hidden stump when he tripped." He shrugged his shoulders.

"But that makes no sense." Pearl chewed on her lip. "Pat didn't drink. He hadn't had a drink the whole time he lived here. I would have known...." she trailed off, lost in her thoughts.

"The science doesn't lie; you know that, Pearl. We're waiting for further toxicology results and analysis of his stomach contents, but for now it appears to be nothing more than an unfortunate accident."

Pearl shook her head. She needed to figure out why he had been drinking. Somebody had to know something. And what had happened to the inheritance check?

She interrupted her thoughts. "One other thing I thought of: Did you or the medical examiner find any money or a check on him?"

"No," said the sheriff. "Why?"

"Well, I looked in his shed this morning and I found a letter from an attorney that had had a check for $5,000 attached. But the check was missing. As far as I know, he didn't have a bank account, so where could the money or the check have gone? All I found was $175 in cash and a jar of coins."

The sheriff furrowed his brow. "That is concerning. We'll try to find out if anyone has information about that."

"I would appreciate you looking into it further, Dan. It certainly gave someone a motive for wanting Pat dead. I'll let you know if I find out any more, as well. As for the other money, I'm going to hang onto it for now. Is that okay?"

"Sure. Keep me informed of anything you find out. The sheriff slid his chair back and got up, signaling that the conversation had ended. "Anything else?"

"Not that I can think of right now." Pearl stood and moved the empty jar to the countertop near the refrigerator. She opened the refrigerator door and checked the dates on the four jars of milk inside, selecting the most recent.

"I hope you brought a cooler or something to keep it cold on the way home. I guess I should have mentioned that earlier. If it gets too warm, it will go sour. It's best to carry a cooler in your trunk, so you'll always have a way to keep the milk cold." She handed him the milk. "If you need a cold bag, I can loan you one for tonight."

"That'd be great. I didn't know it could be a problem if I took it straight home." He laughed.

Pearl went back into the kitchen to get an insulated bag out of a drawer for him.

After the sheriff had left Pearl got out another jar of milk and made a hot cocoa to help her sleep. Her brain raced 90 miles an hour, as she began to plot her next steps. *Even if the authorities don't care about a shed boy, I do. I'm going to find out what Pat was doing before he "fell" in the woods and what happened to that check.*

Chapter 4

If Pearl wanted the goats' coats looking halfway decent for the show, she needed to get them clipped right away. She couldn't put it off any longer. She wouldn't bother washing them first because she didn't have a good way to keep them from getting cold, and they didn't seem dirty to her anyway.

Inside the barn, she searched through the drawers and cupboards in the milk room for the tools she needed. Pearl wasn't organized enough to return tools to a specific location after using them—and Pat hadn't been much better—so there was little logic to where to find them. In one cupboard she found the clippers; they were hard to miss because they were in a large black plastic case. She took them from the case, plugged them in the electric outlet, and laid them on top of the little refrigerator next to the milk stand. She also set out the oil and clipper cooling spray, which was used to keep the clippers from overheating and burning the goats' skin.

The pink brush was on the countertop in the milking room where it was easy to grab when she needed to brush an itchy goat. The hoof trimmers, which had to be sharpened frequently because she sometimes used them to cut brush, were also on the counter by the brush. Now Pearl had the equipment needed to get started. She filled the bowl in the milk stand with a cup of goat feed—a custom mix of whole oats, whole barley, black oil sunflower seeds, field peas, and alfalfa pellets—and opened the gate to the main pen. She called to the goats, holding out an unsalted peanut in the shell to lure them over. Jinx, the herd queen, was the first to get there.

Jinx, a white goat with black and brown spots and a little black mustache, jumped onto the milk stand. She was two years old and had been one of Pearl's first goats, along with Kea. Jinx had learned that being on the milk stand guaranteed that she would get food. As she eyeballed the goat, Pearl realized her first mistake. She should have clipped Jinx before she milked her. Clipping a deflated udder would be a challenge, but she had couldn't use that for an excuse to put it off any longer.

Once Jinx's neck was captured in the stanchion and she was munching feed, Pearl turned on the clippers and began to trim. She started with the coat on Jinx's back, going against the grain of the hair. Once she had done the back and sides, she moved to the harder, bony areas over the hips. Being a novice, she left a few bald spots. She was glad she had chosen to get it done this early! Once the back and sides were completed, she moved to the legs, neck and chest areas, taking care to remove all the long hair that hung over the hips and hooves.

Jinx finished her food and began to dance with her back feet. Pearl gave her a little more grain and then moved on to the hard part—the udder. She had to change the blade to a finer one, which would also ensure that it wasn't too hot for this sensitive body part. She lifted each leg to get all the hair around the udder and held onto the teats while she clipped the mammary.

Once finished, she stood back and scrutinized her handiwork. She noticed four or five areas that needed a once-over. She swapped the blade and re-clipped the long hairs. Then she grabbed the brush and brushed all the excess hair off the goat and swept it off the milk stand. At that point, Jinx had had enough and started to stomp her feet. Pearl, ever the procrastinator, decided to defer the hoof trimming until closer to the goat show. After all, she had three more goats to clip.

After her neck was released, Jinx turned, jumped down, and rushed toward the gate, glad to get away. Kea was next, and then the two dry yearlings. Kea, the same age as Jinx, was a buckskin—brown with a black cape and black legs. Pearl found the trimming itself went a little faster as she gradually got the hang of it, but the longer the clippers worked, the hotter they got—which meant stops and starts. Once she had been clipped, Kea had only two semi-bald spots.

The first yearling, Lexi, didn't appreciate grain as much as the milkers did. The black-and-white spotted doeling didn't yet associate the milk stand with food; to her it was a torture device that meant her feet would be handled as Pearl trimmed her hooves. Rather than stand to eat from the bowl, she attempted to lie down, catching her neck in the stanchion while her head twisted sideways and she screamed bloody murder. Pearl had to repeatedly disengage the locking mechanism and lift her by the chest, while pushing her forward to keep her head in the stanchion while she relocked it. At least that allowed the clippers to cool off a little. Pearl found she had to spray them even more often, as well as to brush out the hair buildup on the blade. She was sweating and exasperated by the time she finished clipping Lexi. She was crestfallen when she noticed bald patches on one shoulder and by her tail.

Desi, the white-and gold doe, was the last one to go. Pearl wanted to stop for the day, but forced herself to press on. It took her a good 10 minutes to catch the speedy little critter and drag her into the milk room. While she could lift the recalcitrant 60-pound doe onto the milk stand, her back protested against it with a symphony of pain. Pearl winced at the physical pain, as well as the emotional pain she felt at losing Pat—who should have been there doing the heavy lifting.

Desi seemed more content to eat grain than Lexi had been. She stood still, but she wolfed it down as if she were starved. Then she began to choke. Pearl removed the grain bowl. Desi gagged and disgorged grain and saliva, while Pearl wondered about a Heimlich maneuver for goats. Once Desi quit choking and started breathing normally, Pearl put the bowl back and resumed clipping. She was relieved that a smaller goat meant a smaller surface area to be trimmed. She finished in record time.

Pearl stood back and viewed her handiwork. She was learning; this goat appeared smoother than the others, not counting the too-bushy hair on her face. *Good enough,* thought Pearl.

Buckley nervously trailed Pearl from room to room as she showered, fixed her hair as best she could, and put on a maroon velvet dress and some plain black flats. He knew she was getting ready to go somewhere and he didn't know whether he would be going along or staying home.

Pearl set out a small marrow bone from the freezer. She usually gave one to Buckley just before she left so he would forget about being abandoned. Once he smelled the bone, he acted like he couldn't wait for her to leave soon enough. He settled in front of the counter and made an intermittent whining sound, which added to the agitation she felt about spending time with her sister.

Pearl and her sister Ruby had been planning this dinner at the King Estate Winery for months now. They got together several times a year because they were the only family they had left. They had attended a musical for their last get-together, which Pearl thought was ideal because they didn't have to talk much.

Pearl drove into Veneta, then headed south on Territorial Highway, toward the winery. Ruby was coming from the other direction in town.

The winery is among the finest in the area. It encompasses 1000 acres of grapes, along with an acre of lavender and 30 acres of organic produce. The restaurant uses local food prepared by an outstanding chef. Pearl could rarely afford such a fancy place.

Her mind wasn't on the dinner as she drove into the country past fir trees and fields of cattle, sheep, and goats. She had to get to the bottom of why Pat had started drinking and what he had died from. She believed the sheriff's office had wrapped things up too quickly, calling it an accident. *Could what seemed to her a hasty judgment have anything to do with his social status—recently homeless and now just a shed boy?* She had nothing against the sheriff himself—he seemed like a nice man—but she had seen too many in law enforcement judge poor people harshly.

Her thoughts switched to her date with Ruby. Pearl felt apprehensive. While they made the effort to get together, their lifestyles were worlds apart and the conflict between them usually manifested at some point during each of these events. Pearl saw Ruby as a know-it-all who could come across as brusque even as she appeared oblivious to how others perceived her. She often got her feelings hurt—which turned into anger—when people, rightfully, got defensive with her.

About 45 minutes later, Pearl missed the right turn to the winery because she was distracted by a herd of Boer goats across the road. She drove to the next farm and turned around, backtracked, and headed up the hill to the restaurant. She continued past the restaurant and parked in the lot to the right.

Ruby was already seated at a table waiting for her. The dining area featured a view that overlooked acres of neatly laid out grapevines. Ruby was, as usual, dressed to the nines in a royal blue dress and matching heels. She was heavily made up and awash in jewelry, as though she were attending a fancy ball. Their mother had also been obsessed with jewelry—hence their names.

While Ruby had followed in their mother's footsteps, Pearl had gone the opposite direction. In her experience, women who bedecked themselves in jewels and makeup were insecure but narcissistic. And what a waste of money, not to mention the detrimental impact on the environment caused by mining.

Ruby and Pearl exchanged a few pleasantries and then the waiter arrived at their table with menus and ice water.

"How are things on the farm?" asked Ruby as she glanced at her menu. "Any new babies born?"

"Ruby, the goats are bred in the fall and winter and have kids 150 days later, in the spring or summer. I don't suppose you could have heard, but Buckley found Pat's body when we were taking our daily hike with the goats the day before yesterday. Are you having wine?" Pearl had already selected the King Estate Pinot Gris.

"What? Pat's body? How would I have heard? I can't believe you aren't more upset! What happened?" Ruby raised her eyebrows in shock.

"Oh, I *am* upset. But what can I do about it? The sheriff's office has already ruled it accidental. They say he

43

was drinking and fell and hit his head, but I think there's more to it than that. I think I'm going to have the pinot gris."

"I'm just going to have water, not wine. Why do you think there's more to the story if it was already ruled an accident?" She fingered the gaudy diamond pendant around her neck.

"Well, for one, Pat didn't drink. I happen to know that he hadn't had a drink in years. He had also just inherited some money, which has gone missing. He wasn't sick and he wasn't clumsy. So tripping and hitting his head makes no sense." Pearl furrowed her brow. "He had walked that trail several times a week for over a year. And he was using a flashlight. He made it safely over that fallen log, but then fell on a flat part of the path? I just have a bad feeling about it and I'm going to ask around to find out who would kill him."

"So now you're a detective who knows more than the police?" asked Ruby. She tittered.

Pearl took a deep breath as she started to seethe inside. *Don't let her get to you,* she told herself. "No. I just think they missed something and I want to find out what. They don't know Pat's history like I do."

"What are you going to do now? I knew that bringing a homeless person in to help you wouldn't end well. You can't run that farm by yourself. I told you that you were getting in over your head when you bought it. Why a woman who is almost 60 years old would think she could handle a farm and livestock is beyond me." Ruby shook her head. "I don't know why any woman would want to get dirty doing that kind of work anyway."

Pearl bristled. "I can do whatever I set my mind to. And I enjoy working with the goats and chickens and I like living in the mountains. Why do you always have to throw cold water on everything I do? It isn't like you have the most meaningful life. Anyway, I'll find someone else to help me. Did I tell you I'm planning to show my goats at the Lane County fairgrounds in a few weeks?"

"I'm raising a daughter. That's meaningful. Besides, I'm just looking out for you," Ruby said, twisting the ruby bracelet on her wrist. "You're my little sister. I'd hate for you to be disappointed. You should be trying to find a man who will marry you, not just someone to live in a shed and do farm chores."

Ruby was a year older than Pearl and their mother had pitted them against each other from day one. Ruby was studious and got the best grades. She lorded it over others in high school, while Pearl had been the black sheep. Pearl had no doubt that she was intelligent, but since Ruby had already taken smart (or had it assigned by their mother) she chose wild. Pearl had a zest for life. She liked variety and excitement.

She had chosen not to go to college right after high school. She instead had biked around Europe and spent two years serving in the Peace Corps in South America and another year on a commune that ran an organic farm. She considered herself a hippie at heart. While in the Peace Corps, Pearl realized that she enjoyed providing health care to people with few resources. After she settled down, she went to nursing school, where she was in the top of her class. Their father had been a doctor, so she was following in his medical footsteps. She missed his emotional support. While Ruby and their mother were like two peas in a pod, Pearl and her father had found their own bond. Pearl knew that he would have supported what she was doing with her life if he had lived to see it.

Ruby—who was supposed to be so promising—had dropped out of college after three years, when she found the orthodontist who could keep her supplied in designer clothes and jewelry. She had her mother's blessing, but her father was disappointed that she had not lived up to her potential.

"What day is the goat show? Maybe we can come and watch. Scheherazade likes goats." Ruby took a drink of water.

Pearl wasn't so sure about Scheherazade liking goats. Scheherazade was 16 years old and Pearl thought Ruby was ruining her just like their mother had done to Ruby. Pearl regretted that she hadn't taken the time during Scheherazade's early years to develop a relationship with her. They weren't close at all and the girl was practically grown and out of the house. The one time she had visited Pearl's farm, she worried about breaking a nail or getting her clothes soiled, so she just admired the goats from a distance. The family didn't even have any house pets because they believed animals were dirty and didn't belong indoors.

"It's on September 5th in the livestock building at the fairgrounds. The show starts at 10:00 but the standard breeds are shown in the morning and the Nigerians in the afternoon, so come any time after noon. It would be great if you could come and watch. I could use the moral support and you would probably learn something." *I can get my digs in, too.*

"Well, I hope you can manage without your shed boy," said Ruby disapprovingly, as she unwrapped her napkin and arranged the silverware.

Pearl was never prepared for these jabs and found it best to just let it go or change the subject as soon as possible. "Have you decided what you're going to order? I'm going to get the summer salad and the salmon."

"I'm having the salmon, too, along with the beet salad and pureed potatoes." Ruby took one last glance at her menu and set it aside.

"I'm so glad we finally came here," said Pearl. "The weather is perfect and I can hardly wait to taste the food and wine." Her mouth watered. "So tell me what you've been up to, Ruby."

"Well, Tony is super busy. It seems like everyone is getting orthodontics these days and apparently everyone has found out that he's the best orthodontist in town, so he can barely keep up. Scheherazade is taking AP classes at South Eugene High School. She's planning to go to Stanford, so she knows how important it is to take the right classes and get good grades."

Classic, thought Pearl. *Ask her about what she's been up to and all she has to say is what her husband and daughter are doing. No wonder she thinks raising dairy goats is such hard work. All she ever does is shop and act superior to other people without actually accomplishing anything.*

"That sounds great," said Pearl, forcing herself to sound pleasant. "Have you done anything fun lately?"

"We flew down to LA last week to go shopping. Do you like this silk blouse I got? I got it in six different colors. I bought Scheherazade some new school clothes, too." Ruby beamed. "We're planning to have a family vacation in Hawaii for Christmas."

"That sounds nice." Pearl breathed a sigh of relief as the waiter arrived to take their order. Soon they could talk about the delicious food and avoid anything personal. Sometimes it was hard to believe they were even from the same family.

Chapter 5

Morning chores took longer that day because Pearl had to clean the chicken coop. She felt negligent about not keeping up with it. When she first got chickens, she cleaned the coop every month, like clockwork. But now it had been two months since she had done it, and the coop was a mess because the chickens had started their fall molt. In addition to the bedding and chicken manure, feathers had begun to accumulate. *Oh, well,* she thought, *at least I remembered to get them dried mealworms for the extra protein.*

She grabbed the shovel, garden cart, and broom and headed for the coop, while Buckley trailed along behind. The chickens would be happy to be let out a little early; she hoped none of the girls had to lay an egg while she worked. She didn't want to have to start hunting for nests in the woods like she had last year, after she drove a hen off the nest. She eventually found one with 22 eggs in it! Not knowing which were the oldest or even how old they were, she had thrown them in the compost. Other chicken owners had related stories about being sure a chicken had been killed by a raccoon or fox, only to have it appear three weeks later with several dozen chicks in tow.

The cure for surreptitious nest-making was several days of lockup to get the hen back into the routine of laying in the nests. Pearl hoped she wouldn't have to do that again.

Pearl took pride in cleaning the coop. She had no plans to delegate the job to anyone else. Pat had refused to do it, anyway. He had complained that chickens stink; but Pearl wryly observed that it didn't stop him from eating their eggs. She was more than happy to keep the jobs of egg-gathering and coop cleaning for herself.

She threw some six-grain scratch and dried mealworms onto the ground outside the coop and fenced run to lure the chickens out once the doors were open. Then she opened the door to the covered chicken run, stepped in and opened the flap door over the nests that led to the chicken run. As she walked out and around the coop to the side door, the rooster and five hens began to jump down from their roosts onto the shelf above the nests and then into the run. Pearl used the tall side door to enter the coop and clean it without having to bend over.

Before she could grab the shovel and broom, she had to figure out why only five hens had come out. She had counted them, like usual, the night before and they had all been there. She looked in to see a banty cross on the nest. So much for her timetable. Rather than force a laying hen out, she would have her second cup of coffee.

"C'mon, Buckley. We're taking a break just now. One of the chickens isn't cooperating."

They ambled back to the house and she poured her second cup of coffee, added milk, and put it in the microwave. The microwave hadn't even completed the minute of reheating when Buckley let out a loud series of barks. She peeked out the front window and saw the sheriff's car pulling up.

"Dan, how are you doing? What brings you here?" Pearl opened the door wide. Buckley eagerly jumped at his shin. "Would you like a cup of coffee? I was just going to have one myself. It's no trouble to make it."

"That would be great." He removed his hat and followed her into the house, with Buckley on his heels. She noticed he held an empty, clean half-gallon jar and the cold pack she had loaned him.

"I'm here to get some more goat milk," he continued as he put the jar on the table and sat in a chair. Buckley leaped into his lap without waiting for any encouragement.

"Let me get the coffee going and then we can talk." She extracted two scoops of coffee from the bag, ground them, and added them to a clean filter. Then she rinsed out the pot and filled it to the four-cup line. After flicking the on button, she walked to the table and sat next to the sheriff.

"Have you heard anything else about Pat? Has anything changed?"

The sheriff stroked Buckley's back. "Nothing yet. We are still waiting on toxicology results."

"Have you interviewed anyone to learn more about his last day?" She bit her cuticle.

"I went to the Armadillo Café to talk to Vern and Lorena. They told me that Pat had eaten there in the afternoon and seemed fine at the time. They weren't aware of the inheritance check or that he might have had a lot of money. I've been too busy with traffic stops and out-of-control tweakers to interview anyone else, but my deputy or I will eventually get to it." He raised his eyebrows. "Why?"

Pearl took her heated cup of coffee out of the microwave, then opened the cupboard and removed a mug stamped with *Ruminations: The Nigerian Dwarf Goat Magazine* for the sheriff. She poured the sheriff a cup of the fresh black coffee and put it on the table in front of him.

"Do you want goat milk in your coffee?" she asked with a smile.

"Thanks. I take it black," he responded.

"The reason I asked is that I'm still having trouble coming to terms with the manner of death and the missing check or money—if he actually cashed it." She hung her head. "I'm going into town this afternoon to talk to some people to see if anyone else saw him that day or night or knows anything."

"That's fine, but be careful. If there's evidence of a crime, it's up to us to investigate. Let me know if find out anything relevant. Personally, I think you're barking up the wrong tree." Buckley gazed at him lovingly.

Frustrated, Pearl let out a sigh. "I will."

She finished her coffee, then took the clean jar and put it in the cupboard. She opened the refrigerator door and searched through the jars of milk to find a recent one. She pulled out a half gallon from two days previous. She set it on the table in front of the sheriff.

"Thanks." He stood up, which caused Buckley to jump to the floor. He put on his hat. "I did like you suggested and

I have an ice chest in my car along with a couple of cold packs."

Pearl smiled. She opened the front door and noticed a van coming up the driveway. It was Westin.

"Have you met Westin?" she asked the sheriff. "He's a friend of Pat's. He sometimes does work around the farm when it's something Pat can't handle, like building. He came back into town from the coast a few days ago and he's going to help me get the goats to the goat show."

Westin pulled up at the barn, then sauntered over to the house as the sheriff got into his car. Buckley flew off the porch and raced to meet him.

"What's going on?" Westin mumbled as he walked to the sheriff's car window, then bent down to pick up Buckley.

"I was just getting some of Pearl's famous goat milk." The sheriff studied Westin. "I don't think I know you."

"Westin Denton. I'm a friend of Pearl's. I help her around the farm sometimes. I thought maybe you were here about Pat. Is there anything new on his case?"

"No, it still looks like an accident." The sheriff turned on the ignition. "See you later, Pearl. Nice to meet you, Westin."

Pearl and Westin watched him drive down the driveway and turn onto the highway.

"What's up?" asked Pearl.

"I decided to check in again and see if you needed anything and find out when I need to be here to help you get things loaded for the goat show." He patted Buckley's head.

"If you could help me load the milk stand and goats on the 5th, that would be a huge help. I'm glad it's just one day. I would have liked to go to the Oregon State Fair with them, but I didn't think I could manage being gone that long."

"Sure. Whatever you need. Would you mind if I took a shower here the night before?" he asked.

"Of course I wouldn't. I was going to ask you if you needed to use the shower today," said Pearl. She noticed his dark, curly hair was flat and greasy where it stuck out from the edges of his baseball cap.

Westin looked sheepish. "No, I'm going to stay with my cousin in town tonight and I can get a shower there. Have you eaten yet?"

"No. I was just getting ready to clean the chicken coop when Dan, I mean the sheriff, showed up." As though on cue, a chicken began to cluck loudly to announce that she had just laid an egg. They both turned toward the coop to see a black chicken fly out the door and then run toward the barn to find the rest of the flock.

"No, I haven't eaten. I was planning to go into town later, but I need to get this chicken coop cleaned right now."

After Westin left, Pearl put on her coveralls and returned to the chicken coop to finish the job she had started in the morning. She checked the nests and found three eggs, which she took into the house and added to the open carton on the counter.

She stationed the garden cart at the coop door, then stepped in and began to scoop shovels full of wood shavings, feathers, and chicken poop into it. Once filled, she hauled it over to a place under the trees to turn into compost. She turned and pushed the cart back to the coop and repeated the process. As she started back to the area where she had dumped the first load, she saw Buckley already there, rolling around. His white coat was coated with straw, pine shavings, feathers, and chicken poop.

"Buckley! Stop it, you little brat! Now look at your coat!" He ran toward her, oblivious of the debris that covered his long hair. "Get away! You stink."

It took about four carts to get all the dirty bedding, including the old straw in the nests. Pearl took the broom and swept the finer debris out the door. She was finished. She had given up on trying to keep Buckley out of the mess. After the first roll-around, she knew he would be getting a bath.

She got a bag of pine shavings from the barn to use for fresh bedding for the chickens, along with a few flakes of clean wheat straw for the nests. Buckley trotted along, proudly carrying a large tail feather from the rooster.

Once the coop had been refreshed, Pearl breathed a sigh of relief. She surveyed the coop, chastising herself for avoiding the chore when the results felt so rewarding.

The feed store closed in three hours, so she had to hurry to get Buckley bathed and dried. He always like to go along. Pearl grabbed him, brushed off as much of the hay and debris as possible, and carried him into the house. She tried to breathe through her mouth to avoid the stench. She wanted to hold her nose but needed both hands. She grabbed a towel and deposited Buckley in the utility sink, where she began to run warm water.

Thirty minutes later, after washing, blow-drying, and brushing, Buckley looked again like his fluffy white self. Pearl took off her coveralls and muck boots and checked her reflection in the mirror to make sure she looked semi-presentable. She brushed a few pieces of straw out of her hair—good enough. She grabbed her purse and Buckley and scurried to the car. She couldn't risk letting him get dirty again after all that work. Once she opened the car door, Buckley leaped from her arms into the driver's seat and then into the back of the car. She got in the driver's seat.

Pearl opened the hatchback and arranged the blue tarp in her Subaru Forester. She knew she should have brought her van because she had sworn she wouldn't ruin the Subaru with hay. She preferred to use the more efficient vehicle today, though. She could haul one bale of hay by putting a large tarp in the back, which overlapped onto the seat and up the sides. That kept it free from all but a few pieces of hay, which she could later vacuum out.

She opened the passenger door, lifted Buckley out, and carried him up the wooden ramp and into the store. Pearl inhaled the sweet smell of fresh hay. She noticed bright-colored goat-themed flags that had been added to the décor, but squelched the urge to buy some on impulse. She steered clear of the baby chicks that peeped under the heat lamps above cages in the store's center aisles. She didn't want to be tempted. She eyed the shelves in front of the door that displayed onion and garlic bulbs for fall planting, but passed on them, too.

Pearl walked through the aisles searching for collars. Buckley strained in her arms when they passed the dog treats, so she selected a vegetarian chewy for him. She found the show collars and selected four medium-sized silver choke collars for the does, along with a couple of short leads. Full-sized goats didn't need leads, but unless a child or very short person was showing them, Nigerian Dwarves did.

"Pearl!" said a voice behind her.

She turned toward the voice. Zora Vega stood with her hands on her hips. Zora was heavy and mousy-looking, with a limp brown ponytail. She fancied herself a goat expert and would let no one forget it. She wore jeans, a white polo shirt with *Middle Pass Minis* embroidered on the left side, and filthy muck boots. Zora had had some luck with goat competitions in the past but, to hear her talk, she had the best Nigerian Dwarfs in the state. Pearl found Zora and her passive-aggressive husband insufferable.

Pearl had met Zora at the local goat club. Sarah, another member, let her know that Zora was telling everyone that the goats Pearl had bought were inferior. Just the thought made Pearl huffy. *Zora just loved to stir the pot.*

Pearl knew her goats were of good quality, and it would be proven when she won at the goat show. She had reviewed websites to learn which farms were winning goat shows and goat magazines to learn which ones were the top milkers. She had also read most of the books in print that she could find on goats and goat care. She had ultimately chosen Nigerians and, after deciding on a herd known to have superior stock, she had made the trip to Southern Oregon to purchase two doelings from them.

"Oh, hi, Zora. I'm just getting a few last-minute things for the goat show. Are you going this year?" Pearl gritted her teeth.

Zora rolled her eyes. "Of course I'm going! I won grand champion senior doe at the Lane County Fair this year. My Middle Pass Minis Tootsie Roll is outstanding. My junior does did really well, too. I was surprised you didn't show your goats there."

"I wasn't ready yet. This will be my first goat show. Excuse me," she said as she moved to the front of the counter to make her purchases. Zora followed along behind her, not getting the hint.

"One bale of alfalfa, the chewy, and these collars and leads," she said to the young man running the cash register. He had dreadlocks, large earrings that stretched his earlobes, a nose ring, and the loose and comfy clothing of a modern age hippie. He rang the purchases as Zora interrupted—"I heard you lost your farmhand."

Pearl put Buckley on the counter while she paid. She leaned against the counter to block him from falling or jumping. After he rang up her purchases, the clerk handed her change and receipt—which she dropped into her pocket—and a paper bag that held her purchases. She clutched Buckley with her free arm.

"I'll get your hay in a minute," said the hippie, with a big smile.

"Thanks. I'll meet you out there."

Pearl stepped away from the counter. "Yes; it was a tragic accident. How did you hear about it?" she said, turning her attention to Zora.

Zora snorted, "Oh, you know, word travels around here. My neighbor was down at the Middle Pass Pub and someone there told him. I know Pat had managed to offend a lot of people around town.

"My neighbor also told me that Dave Miller, who owns the Pub, was mad when Pat started seeing Jane Wilson, since he had been involved with her first. I wonder if he had something to do with it? Personally, I don't know what Jane saw in Pat—or Dave, for that matter, with his coke habit." Zora closed her eyes as she talked, a habit Pearl found irritating.

"Hmm," Pearl said, not wanting to give anything away to Zora, but filing the information in her brain.

"Are you going to be able to handle getting all your goats to the fairgrounds without Pat to help you?" Zora smirked.

"Oh, that's not a problem. I have plenty of friends who can help me," lied Pearl, biting her cuticle absentmindedly, then pulling it away from her mouth, embarrassed. *Anyone is better than that scrawny little husband she's always ordering around.*

"Oh, I'm glad to hear that," said Zora, gushing. "The more competition the better. We need to make our minimum numbers so our wins count. I'd better get going now. I have so much to do. At least I don't have to clip the goats, since I already did it for the Lane County Fair."

Buckley struggled in Pearl's arm. *Even he doesn't like Zora,* thought Pearl. "I have to get going, too, if I'm going to get anything done today. See you at the fairgrounds." She turned and walked out the door before Zora could respond.

As Pearl drove home, she obsessed about Zora's comment regarding Dave and Jane. Tomorrow she would go to the Pub to find out if Pat had been there that night and if he had any money. Maybe that's where he had been drinking. And at the same time, she would find out what Dave had to say about his breakup with Jane.

But that would have to wait until morning. It was common knowledge that the Pub could be unpleasant at night, with bikers and other rough characters there. Pearl didn't want to take any chances.

Chapter 6

The light shone in the window at 6:45 am, waking Pearl. The sun rose an hour later than it had just a few months earlier. She lay in bed, not wanting to get up just yet in the chill morning. Pearl stretched as she made a mental inventory of what she wanted to accomplish that day. Buckley took the stretching as a signal to jump off the bed. The jump signaled Pearl to get up and start the day before the little furball leaped back up to hassle her.

By the time she finished her first cup of coffee, chores, and breakfast, Pearl had made up her mind to go to the Middle Pass Pub that afternoon and talk to Dave Miller.

She walked to the shed carrying a two white plastic garbage bags and an empty box to put items in. She again entered, and Buckley trailed along behind her.

"There's no reason I can't get rid of the stuff no one else would want," she said to herself.

She started by emptying the little refrigerator into a garbage bag, except the cans of fizzy water, which she set aside. With no idea how old the food was, she would assume it was all inedible and throw it away. She unplugged the empty fridge. *No need to pay for unnecessary electricity.* She shooed Buckley away from a to-go container he was pawing and dropped it in the garbage bag. She gathered all the other leftover to-go containers and added them to the bag. After she checked for mold, Pearl set aside the bread to feed to the chickens when she was done. Buckley sniffed at the bread on the table.

Next, she gathered the clothing strewn around the room and in the drawers and put it in the second garbage bag. She stripped the bed and removed the pillowcase from the pillow. She stuffed the bedding in the bag with the clothes. She would wash it all and donate the clothing to White Bird Clinic, a nonprofit organization that distributes clothing to people who are homeless. It seemed a fitting choice for a donation.

Pearl sorted through the mail on the table again. She tossed junk mail into the garbage bag with the food. She had eliminated all the food with the potential to go bad and gathered up the clothing and bedding to wash. She would load anything was left into the box when she came back to finish cleaning. Pearl took the two garbage bags and the leftover bread, and closed up the shed. Buckley walked alongside, intrigued by the food bag and bread.

Pearl put the garbage bags on the ground. She walked to the chicken coop and opened the bread bag, then broke each slice into smaller pieces, calling "Chicken. Chicken. Chicken."

The chickens rushed out from under trees and across the yard to eat the bread, but before they could get there, Buckley had wolfed down several pieces. Pearl grabbed him. "Buckley, no!"

She held the struggling pup under one arm, clutched the bag with trash in her other hand, and walked over to the metal garbage can next to the house. She dropped the trash bag in. She returned to the bag of clothing and linens and grasped it in her now-empty hand. She climbed the steps and entered the house, where she placed the bad dog and bag of clothing on the floor.

She took the bag of laundry into the back room, opened the washing machine lid, poured in liquid laundry detergent and dumped the bedding and clothes in on top, and set it for hot water wash.

In the kitchen, Pearl poured the coffee left in the pot into her cup, added a generous share of goat milk to it, and put the mug in the microwave. She took the mug of hot liquid and plopped in a chair at the dining room table. Buckley stepped into his dog bed and curled into a ball. He faced the wall, miffed after being denied the leftover food carton and stale bread.

She was about halfway through her coffee when Buckley leaped into the air, ran toward the door, and began to yap. Pearl glanced out the window and saw the sheriff walk up the steps.

Is he out of milk already? I wonder if he has some news regarding Pat's death?

"Good morning, Dan. What brings you out here today?" asked Pearl apprehensively.

"I was in the area, so I decided to stop in and update you on a few more things we've found so far about Pat's death. Can I come in?"

"Coffee or tea?" Pearl opened the door wide and let him in as Buckley jumped against his legs in excitement. They sat down at the dining table.

"No, thanks. I don't plan to stay long. I already told you about his blood alcohol. The medical examiner also determined that the injury on his head was accidental and there were no other injuries, other than a few bruises and scratches he probably got when he fell. He did note that Pat had high potassium in his blood, but as you probably know, that could be caused by chronic kidney problems. Do you know anything about his medical history?"

"Other than that he was an alcoholic who didn't drink, I knew nothing about his medical history. He seemed healthy enough. He was one of those people, mainly men, who refuse to see a doctor, for fear they might find something wrong with them and 'get sucked into the medical system.'"

"Well, that's all we know for now. We'll know more after the autopsy is completed. Have you talked to anyone in town yet?"

"No, I've been too busy getting ready for the goat show and doing work around here," said Pearl. He didn't ask if she *planned* to talk to anyone.

Dan suppressed a grin. "It's just as well. I'm glad you have something else to keep you occupied," he said.

Pearl parked down the street from the Middle Pass Pub. She walked past the fabric store, the Ace Hardware store, and the bail bonds office, which was appropriately located right next to the Pub, and entered the front door.

The drinking establishment was styled after an English pub, with a large fireplace and long tables with benches that encourage strangers to sit together. Smaller groups could sit around the fireplace in big, comfy leather chairs. The walls contained numerous pictures of the countryside and English mansions. The centerpiece of the pub was a beautiful old carved wooden bar with about 10 barstools along the counter.

Pearl surveyed the smattering of patrons, clutching her purse close to her body. She had her guard up because the Pub had a reputation as a rough place. That didn't seem true of the daytime clientele, though. Three old men perched at the far end of the bar—probably regulars. What appeared to be businesspeople, because they wore suits, were seated around the fireplace in the chairs. The benches were all empty.

The bartender that day was a young 20-something woman with a short pixie haircut. She wore a hot pink leather miniskirt, with a tight T-shirt inked with "Middle Pass Pub" on a drawing of a Nonic pub glass, and black mock-leather knee-high boots.

Pearl walked to the bar and made eye contact with her. "How can I help you?" the bartender queried Pearl as she wiped a glass she had removed from the dishwasher.

"I'm looking for Dave. Is he working today?" Pearl turned and glared at the old men at the end of the bar who were staring at her.

"He's in the office right now. Like, who should I say is asking for him?" She placed the glass on the shelf with the clean ones and chose another.

"My name is Pearl Kelly. I wanted to talk to him about Pat Steinberg." Pearl climbed onto a barstool and turned to scowl at the old men, who suddenly found something to talk about among themselves.

The pixie finished drying the second glass and put it on the shelf. "Back in like a second. I'll go get him."

She came back with Dave trailing behind her. He was overmuscled, with big arms and a small waist accentuated by the tight T-shirt he wore. His hair had started to thin, so he shaved his head but made up for it with a groomed mustache and beard. His superficial charm and macho look made him a hit with the women in town.

Pearl noticed a 9mm Glock in a small holster on his hip. She snorted. *Why does a big, strong man need to carry a firearm all the time?* She knew it wasn't uncommon in a lot of rural areas in Oregon, but still thought it was ridiculous.

"Hi, Pearl. I'm sorry to hear about Pat. How are things on the farm?" he asked. "We can sit over here." He led the way past the bar to the far corner of the room here they could sit in two roomy chairs. "Did you want something to drink?"

Pearl thought for a moment. "I'd like a glass of pinot noir. Or whatever the house red is."

66

"Gina, can we get a Black Butte porter and a house pinot noir, please?" Dave yelled across the room. The people by the fireplace turned and stared for a minute and then returned to whatever they had been talking about. Dave sniffed and pulled out one of the chairs for her. The strong cologne that wafted off his body made Pearl feel like gagging.

They settled into the chairs and Gina brought their drinks and a bowl of Twiglets. When she was out of earshot, Pearl said, "So, did you hear how Pat died?"

"Yeah. I heard it was an accident. He fell in the woods near your farm? I felt bad for the guy. I know he could be a jerk at times, but I kind of felt sorry for him because he was so goofy. He was proud of his job on your farm, though." He rubbed his nose.

"Was he here that day or night?" She sipped her wine. "What vineyard is this from?"

"Bennett Vineyards. They're down in Cheshire. We like to serve local alcohol when we can." Dave took a swig of beer. "Pat was here that evening. I remember because he usually drank Sierra Mist, but that night he wanted a real drink. We were celebrating the money he got from his inheritance. I assume you knew about that."

"I knew his uncle had died and he was going to get something, but I just found out that it was a lot of money — for him, anyway — when I discovered the letter from the lawyer in his room. Do you know how much he got?" Pearl gazed at him intently.

Dave peered around the room, snuffled, and then lowered his deep, baritone voice. He leaned back and jiggled his right leg. "I think everyone in the pub knew about it that evening because he couldn't keep his mouth shut. He didn't have a bank account to deposit it in, and he didn't want a paper trail, so he had asked me if I could cash it and give him the money. He didn't want it to affect his food assistance money." Dave rubbed his hands together.

"I ran it through the Pub's account and gave him the $5,000 that afternoon. He was in a hurry to get home but insisted on buying me a scotch and soda. We each had one—to celebrate," he said." Dave took a deep breath and then let it out with a loud exhale.

"So, as far as you know, he still had most of the money when he left?" Pearl wrinkled her brow.

"He certainly didn't spend much in here." Dave laughed.

"Did he have any more alcohol after the celebratory drink?" asked Pearl.

"He complained about a stomachache when he was here. That was part of his rationale for the drink. He claimed that scotch and soda would cure an upset stomach. But he only had the one drink and I seen him leave around 5:30 or 6:00. I know it was before dark. He left the same time as Joe. Said he was going home. I didn't leave until closing that night so I know he didn't come back in later." Dave stroked his dark mustache, studied the room, then sniffed again.

68

Pearl sipped her wine. *Was Dave desperate enough to kill Pat for money? It might not be beyond the realm of possible if he had a cocaine addiction.*

"When they found him, he didn't have any money on him," she said, watching Dave intently. "The police didn't release that information because they didn't even know about the inheritance. That's why I'm suspicious. But according to Sheriff Springer, the death was accidental. They say he fell and hit his head."

Dave rubbed his hands on his legs. "Are you thinking someone attacked him and robbed him?"

"I wonder. Who is this Joe who left at the same time as Pat? Do you know anything about him? Does he live around here? Do you know if he heard Pat talking about the money?" Pearl chewed her lip.

"Joe Martinez. Hispanic guy. Flannel and jeans kind of guy. He's a logger who lives out in Deadwood. He's a regular here, drinks a lot and has been in a few times since then, acting perfectly normal. I know he lent Pat some money a while back. He had been whining about not being able to buy his kid a bike for his birthday because he had no money." Dave finished his beer with a gulp, setting the glass down hard. He took a handkerchief from his shirt pocket and blew his nose.

"Do you know if Pat paid him back?"

"I have no idea." Dave looked down at the table and started to jiggle his leg again.

"Maybe you could keep an eye on him for me and tell me if he's flashing any cash around. In the meantime, I need to talk to him. Thanks for your help, Dave. Please don't say anything to anyone else." Pearl finished her wine.

"One more thing I just remembered. Did you use to date Jane Wilson?"

He sniffed, then let out a nervous laugh. His leg jiggling accelerated. "Yeah, we went out for a while. Why?"

"How did it end?" She raised her eyebrows.

"She dumped me." He sniggered, then sniffed again. "I had heard she was with Pat, but I never seen them together. I don't care, though. I have no problem in the girlfriend department." He began to crack his knuckles.

"Okay, I was just checking because I had heard different stories. Thanks for all your help," said Pearl. They both got up and Dave strutted back to the office as Pearl started toward the door.

A thought crossed her mind. She walked up to the bar and sat on the stool nearest where Gina stood. "Gina, were you working here last Friday night?

"Yeah, my shift was from 5:00 pm to 2:00 am. Why?"

"Do you remember whether Dave was here all evening until the bar closed?"

Gina paused, thinking. "Yeah, except for when we, like, ran out of Fireball whiskey. For some reason everyone was drinking Fireball that night. He had to go all the way to a Eugene liquor store, because, like, it was too late to go to one in Junction City or Veneta. They close earlier."

"Do you know what time he left?"

"I think he left, like, a little after 7:00 and got back around 9:00. Why?"

"Oh, I'm just trying to figure out the timeline for Pat's death and what he was doing before that." Pearl was purposely vague because she didn't want Gina to suspect anything. "Thanks for your help."

Pearl slid off the barstool and headed out the door, ignoring the eyes that followed her.

Chapter 7

I need to talk to Jane again, thought Pearl as she sat on the front porch the next morning after her chores. *I wonder if she even knows about Pat?* Pearl had changed into her black jeans, a T-shirt that said "Well-behaved women rarely make history," and goat-patterned socks under her Crocs.

Buckley crouched in front of the porch snapping and pawing at an insect. Pearl peered closely. A yellowjacket. August and September were the worst time of the year for the nasty little creatures. The prior year she had been stung by three at the same time, after she stepped on a ground nest. She believed they get more aggressive as summer comes to a close.

"Buckley, stop! You'll regret it if you catch one. Come here." He climbed the steps and jumped onto the padded wooden bench beside her, circled three times and lay down.

Pearl had two more days before the goat show. The goats were ready to go, and she had packed the van with items she didn't need before then. She needed Westin to help load the goats. She would still need to clean feed bowls and empty and wash out buckets. She had already ordered bedding for the pens she had paid for.

After what she had learned from Dave last night, Pearl wanted to visit Jane before she left for the fairgrounds. She hoped this time Jane would be straightforward with her about her relationship with Pat. Pearl also wanted to hear Jane's opinion of Dave, his honesty, and whether he had a propensity for violence.

"Buckley, you stay home this time. I don't think Jane appreciated you in her house last week, and I want to be on my best behavior to get her to talk."

Pearl put Buckley in the house and left by the back door, down the three steps on the wooden porch, and out to the path in the woods. She hadn't taken the goats out since they found Pat's body. She needed to get back into the habit for the sake of the goats' health and her own, but for now it triggered her just to think about going out in the woods.

She jumped the creek, which could use some rain, and continued to Jane's back yard. The brown sugar scent of a Katsura tree welcomed her to the elaborate garden. She hadn't noticed the smell the last time she was there. She couldn't identify the tree, but saw that the leaves had started to turn color. Her eyes were drawn to some colorful chrysanthemums that were still in bloom. Another scent— vanilla from fragrant angel coneflowers—wafted over in competition with the other pleasant odors. *Jane certainly had a green thumb.*

Pearl knocked on the back door, worried that she should have called first. Jane answered the door and gazed out at Pearl. Her open face indicated that she was in a better mood than she had been the last time. "Where's Buckley?"

"I left him at home today. He was a pain the last time, with his muddy paws. He'll be all right. I don't plan to stay long. I wanted to tell you about Pat, if you haven't already heard."

"Come on in and have a cuppa." Jane pushed open the screen, then stepped back and waved her into the house.

"Thanks. I'll just have whatever you're having." Pearl wiped her feet on the rug inside the door and walked through the cluttered mudroom to the dining room.

She sat at the table and noticed that it had a new, clean tablecloth with an autumn leaves pattern and was much less cluttered. She looked up at the wall and saw that Jane had added a new shadowbox to the wall display. This one contained four large seeds.

"Oh, a new shadowbox!" said Pearl. "You're so creative. What is it?"

"Those are pong pong seeds. That half-dead plant by the sink is a failed germination. I was thinking it was just a slow starter, but I probably need to throw it away. They grow into the trees, like the one out back. It's in the west side of the garden in a pot because I have to bring it in during the cold weather. It's a tropical plant. *Cerbera odallam* is the scientific name.

"The Garden Club gets catalogs from all over the world—exotic plants and such. They're freely available to members who are interested in growing hard-to-find or exotic plants. I think that's where I first learned about them. The tree is the one in my exotic plant area with the orange fruits." Jane beamed.

"Is it one with the incredible smell?" asked Pearl. "Something really sweet hit me when I came into the garden."

"No. They don't have a noticeable odor. It could have been the coneflowers you smelled. Anyway, I ordered the seeds online from a nursery in Thailand because I wanted to try growing the trees. One of the seeds I planted turned into a tree—or, actually, more of a bush at this point—and the other one didn't survive. I had the seeds sitting on a bowl on my table and someone stole two of them, apparently during the garden club tour." Jane looked irritated. She put the kettle on the stove and got out two cups and teabags.

"Wow, that's rude! So people came into your house?" Pearl watched Jane's sudden swirl of activity.

"I felt like I had to let them use the bathroom because the tour took hours and it only seemed humane," Jane said with disgust, as she pulled out a chair and sat in it. "Otherwise I wouldn't have done it."

"Why would they steal seeds?" asked Pearl, chewing on her lip.

"I suppose for the novelty. You have to admit they're kind of cool-looking. I was so mad when I discovered them missing. Anyway, I like making shadowboxes, so I decided to frame the ones that were left. I don't need more than the one tree." Jane jumped up just as the kettle began to whistle and poured water in the two cups. She carried them to the table.

"Did they take anything else?" asked Pearl.

"Not that I know of. As you can tell by the clutter, I don't know everything I have." Jane looked around and laughed.

"It took me a few days to even notice that the seeds were missing. I may just rent a porta-potty next year and lock my doors, since obviously some people can't be trusted." Jane shook her head.

"You should come and watch the goat show I'm going to. I've entered four goats," said Pearl on an impulse. She felt herself warming up to Jane. "It's this coming weekend." She cautiously tried her tea. Small sips were safe.

Jane's eyes brightened. "It would be something to do. I've never seen a goat show."

"The show will be in the Lane County Fairgrounds livestock building at 10 o'clock on the 5th but you can come later. I hope you can make it." Pearl tried to discern whether Jane was serious. She wanted people to see her win ribbons.

Pearl took another sip of tea, then continued, "Well, so much for all of that. Did you hear about what happened to Pat?" She paused, watching Jane's face for some sign of emotion.

"No, I haven't heard anything. I haven't even gone anywhere for the last few days. I've just been working around the garden. What happened?" Jane looked puzzled.

A feeling of dread washed over Pearl. "Oh, no. I probably should have called or come over again right after it happened. Anyway, to get to the point, after I was over here that morning, I took the goats for a walk out in the woods and Buckley found Pat's body on the trail behind your house, right by the fork that leads to Crown Road."

Jane's face went white. "He's dead?"

"Yes. Law enforcement has tentatively ruled it an accident, but I don't believe it. I'm trying to figure out what happened. I'm hoping you can help me. I have so many questions. For example, did you know about his inheritance?"

"I did. He had promised to take me out to dinner once he got the money." Jane shifted in her chair.

"So you *were* seeing him. Dave told me." Pearl had avoided accusing her of lying when they talked the last time." He said you dumped him for Pat. Is that right? He acted nonchalant about it."

"Hah!" said Jane. She shook her head. "Nonchalant? He was furious when I dumped him. He thinks he's God's gift to women. Once I learned he used cocaine, I was done. He even offered me some one night. After that, I went home and thought about it. I decided I couldn't be involved with someone who had a drug habit. Not only that, but he's drowning in debt. If he keeps it up, he's going to lose the bar." Jane crossed her arms. She shook her head, disgusted.

"That's interesting, because he told me he cashed the check for Pat with his bar account. Does that seem like something he would do? Do you think he would be capable of killing Pat for money? Or having someone else do it?" Pearl leaned forward, getting more animated as she talked to Jane. "He claims he didn't leave the bar that night, which, if true, would rule him out as the person who killed Pat."

"It wouldn't have cost him anything to cash the check, so he probably did. But do you honestly think someone would kill a person for only $5,000? Especially if they had to split it two ways?" Jane shook her head.

"I guess it depends on how desperate they were," said Pearl. "Do you think he might have been jealous enough to kill Pat, especially considering that he uses drugs? I also found out that Pat had been drinking that night—which was totally out of character for him. Dave said Pat suggested it, but I can't help wondering whether he purposely talked him into drinking so he could take advantage of him and steal his money. But he also said that Pat only had one drink, while the sheriff told me that his blood alcohol was .06. That doesn't add up. He would have had to have more than one drink, but he also wouldn't have been so impaired that he was staggering and falling."

Jane rubbed her eyes. "Dave is definitely sneaky, but he was never violent around me. I do know some locals at the Pub were intimidated by him. I only went out with him for a month or so. And even though it's flattering to think he might have been jealous because I chose Pat over him, I can't see him killing over it. Or for less than $5,000.

"I never knew Pat to drink either, so that part seems strange to me, too. Especially because I thought things were going better for him than they had for a long time." Jane took a deep breath, then teared up.

Pearl continued: "Before I left, I also talked to that young bartender, Gina, who worked that night. Dave claimed he never left that evening, but when I asked her, she remembered that he'd gone to Eugene to get some liquor they ran out of. Coincidentally—or not—he was gone during the very time that the medical examiner estimated Pat had died. That needs to be taken into consideration."

Jane scowled. "Nothing would surprise me about Dave anymore."

"Not to belabor the point about you and Pat ... but I was pretty sure he'd been going over to see you at night because Buckley would start barking every time he was on the back path that leads to your house. He went that way too often and it was too late and out of habit for him to be walking to town."

Pearl took a deep breath when she saw the hurt in Jane's eyes. Jane probably felt even worse than Pearl did about Pat's death because she had been romantically involved with him. "Oh, Jane, I'm so sorry for your loss. I can see that you cared about him as much as I did. What led you to get involved with Pat? You seem so much more accomplished than him."

"He was always nice to me and we could talk about anything. I don't know if you were aware, but he read a lot. Since my husband Eric died, I just get so lonely. It also helps to have a man around to help with some of the work keeping up the garden. I felt safer having a man around. Maybe because I've almost never been alone in my life. I went to college right after I left my parents' home, then I met Eric and we moved in together and were married for 20 years. We did everything together.

80

"I could also see that Pat needed someone to take care of him, too. You know, there isn't a lot to choose from out here." Jane began to sob. "I can't say I was in love with him, but he did make me feel better."

"I know what you mean about being able to talk about anything. I met him in Eugene years ago and I was impressed with his knowledge. He still likes to read and even subscribes to the *New Yorker*. I got acquainted with him and we struck up a friendship, which is how he came to be my shed boy." Pearl considered what Jane had said; perhaps they had more in common than she had thought.

Pearl had an idea. "Will you team up with me to try to find his killer? Despite what the police say, I'm certain someone was behind his death and it wasn't an accident." She felt her outrage return. "I don't think they are taking it seriously because he was just a shed boy!"

Jane winced, then looked at her hard. "It sounds like you think he was less-than, too. Do you hear yourself? Shed boy? Isn't that a little condescending?"

Pearl felt her cheeks reddening. She avoided looking at Jane. "It's just a joke," she muttered.

Jane shook her head. "At whose expense?"

Pearl crossed her arms and changed the subject. "Were you home that night?"

"No, in fact now I feel a little guilty about not being here, since he was found on the path behind my house. Maybe he was on his way over here and I could have prevented it. I spent the night at my sister's in town. We went out to see Little Shop of Horrors at Actor's Cabaret dinner theater. I only got back the morning you came by looking for him." Jane dabbed at her eyes with a tissue.

"Actually, Jane, he'd been headed in the opposite direction—toward town—so I have no idea where he was going. I wonder if he could have tried your house and then decided to go back into town. If he wasn't thinking clearly because of the alcohol … there's one more person I want to talk to. Dave said Pat left the bar at the same time as a guy named Joe Martinez. Joe may have been the last person to see Pat alive. He's a logger from out in Deadwood. Do you know him?"

"I wouldn't say I *know* him but I've talked to him at the Pub a few times. Nice guy, but he drinks too much. One thing I liked about Pat was that he didn't drink. Joe's divorced, but has a son. I think he lives with his mother."

"Thanks; that's useful." Pearl finished her tea and stood. "Please consider helping me find out what happened. Tomorrow I've got to get ready for the goat show, but I'm going to track down Joe Martinez after I get back. I hope you can come to the show! If you come at noon, you can have lunch with us and be in plenty of time to seem me show my goats in the afternoon. It's in the livestock building at the Fairgrounds."

Chapter 8

Pearl thumbed through the Lane County phonebook until she got to Martinez. No Joe, but there was an Isabella and a Doris. Pearl thought Isabella was more likely to be the mother. Doris wasn't a Hispanic name so she was probably his wife. She wrote both names, phone numbers, and addresses on a yellow post-it note and stuck on the dry erase board she used for to-do lists. She would call when she got back from the goat show and then drive out there if she needed to.

She couldn't shake the feeling of unease. Nothing added up, and she wondered if she and Jane were the only ones who understood Pat. Perhaps she should have kept a better eye on him, considering his history. But he was a grown man and she could only do so much to manage him. She knew from experience not to get on his bad side.

"Buckley, let's get the goats and go on a final walk before the show. Everyone needs to work off some energy before being cooped up in a vehicle or small pen and we all need to get back to our normal routines." Buckley wagged his tail and leaped up and down. Pearl removed her slippers and put on her muck boots. She opened the front door and stepped onto the porch. An exuberant Buckley trotted along beside her.

The goats knew the drill, even though it had been a while since they had been allowed out for a walk. Pearl had found it too traumatic to replay that awful day, but she knew she had to get over it and get on with her life. She had depended too much on Pat and if she wanted to be a successful dairy goat farmer, she would have to take on all of the responsibilities.

The goats jostled each other near the gate, then pushed through two at a time once she removed the chain that held it shut and it began to swing open. Buckley raced to the side to avoid being stepped on. They headed directly for the path into the woods, pausing just long enough to grab bites of various plants as they made their way there. Pearl left the gate ajar and followed along behind them. She had to redirect two of the kids that wandered off in a different direction. They trudged along the path, with the goats stopping intermittently to nibble different plants. Buckley dashed ahead as usual.

The hike had been uneventful, other than the progress made by the goats on eradicating the salal along the way and the blackberry leaves in the patch where Pat's body had lain the last time they were hiking. Pearl had spent some of the time throwing a stick for Buckley to fetch, while mulling over what she had learned the day before from Dave and Jane. She needed to put her thoughts about Pat's death aside for now and focus on the goat show, meeting with goat friends, and the fun she would have showing the goats—hopefully winning a few blue ribbons.

Pearl had just gotten the goats back into the barn and was refreshing their water and hay when she noticed the distinct sound of Westin's van. Buckley could always identify that sound. He rushed for the door as the vehicle stopped, and start to whine. Pearl heard the van door slam shut as she got to the barn door. As soon as she opened the door, Buckley scurried out to greet Westin.

"Are you ready for the goat show?" He grinned and scooped up the little dog.

"Nearly," said Pearl. "We just need to load the van tonight and in the morning we can hit the road. I'm a little nervous about showing the goats. I haven't practiced enough, especially with the yearlings. I hope the judge doesn't hold that against me. But it'll be great to see the goat friends I've made over the past year."

"You hungry?" asked Pearl. "I'm going to make my famous macaroni and cheese for supper. I also got some broccoli from Bush Farms to go with it."

Westin's eyes lit up. "That sounds great. Give us the energy we need to work."

"Come up on the porch. You can play with Buckley while we're waiting. I'll bet he'd like that. He loves to have anyone throw his ball."

Pearl started to prepare the meal. She looked outside from time to time to watch Westin and Buckley play. After she got the macaroni and cheese in the oven, she looked out to see them settled on the bench on the porch.

"Would you like a glass of wine while we're waiting?" she asked Westin, as she leaned out the front door.

"Sure. Whatever you are having," he responded. Buckley was curled in a ball next to him. She saw the chickens leisurely making their way toward the coop for the night.

"Would you be so kind as to close up the chickens for me once they all make it into the coop?" asked Pearl. "There are six hens and one rooster." The chickens had started to roost earlier each night, as the days got shorter.

"Sure. No problem," said Westin. He walked to the chicken coop, counted the chickens to make sure they were all there, and closed the man door and the chicken door. He returned to the house as Pearl was setting the table, with Buckley at his heels as he entered the front door.

Pearl set out Buckley's food in an attempt to distract him from begging from her guest. No matter how many times she had told Pat, he had a bad habit of surreptitiously feeding morsels to the little dog. Now Buckley expected to be able to harass any guest into feeding him.

They ate in silence, other than Pearl chiding Buckley from time to time when his begging became too blatant.

Westin patted his stomach. "That was delicious. Can I help you with the dishes?"

Pearl glowed. She loved to feed people, especially when they appreciated the food she prepared. "I hate to turn down an offer of help, but I want to put the dishes off for now. I need to double check on what I need for the show and get the milking done first." She sighed.

"That's okay. I'll wash them for you. I know you have lots to do." Westin stood and started to clear the table.

"Thank you!" she said, surprised by his generosity.

Pearl picked up the copy of *Raising Goats for Dummies* she had taken from the bookcase earlier, sat in the rocking chair, and turned again to the section on showing. She wanted to see if she had missed anything on the supply list that she would need. She had purchased some nylon feed bags to hang on the pens for feeding hay, as well as a couple of extra water buckets so the goats left at home still had some. She remembered bleach to pre-clean the stalls. She didn't want to a risk her goats contracting a disease from prior animals or nearby goats. She grabbed the bleach from the laundry room, where she saw that Pat's clothes and bedding were still in the washing machine. She transferred everything to the dryer and started it.

After moving the clothes from the washer to the dryer, Pearl carried the bleach into the living room. "If you want to hang out with Buckley after you get the dishes done and then watch a movie when I get back, feel free. Are you staying in your van tonight?"

"I have some things to do tonight. I'll be back later and will just stay in my van here then, if you don't mind."

Westin gave Buckley a pat and headed for the door. "See you in the morning."

"Okay, I want to get going by 8:00 am at the latest, so we have to start loading the van at 7:00. See you then."

Pearl approached her desk and pulled from the space between the desk and wall a rolled-up vinyl Hidden Creek Farm banner she had had made for goat events. She knew it wasn't essential for a simple goat show, but this would be the first time she would get to highlight her farm. She took out a handful business cards and a holder as well as the stack of pamphlets she had created entitled "So You Want to Get a Goat"—which had the dual purpose of educating newbies and promoting her herd. The sign, business cards, and brochures all featured her logo, which showed a goat surrounded by purple flowers and a creek in the background.

Pearl had only a few kids to sell this year, but getting her farm name out into the public would be a big help in the future—especially if her goats were winning shows. She also grabbed the notebook with all the goat registration papers from the American Dairy Goat Association (ADGA).

She turned and entered the bedroom to get her show clothes, which consisted of white denim pants and a white polo shirt with Hidden Creek Farm embroidered on the left chest. She laid them out on top of her dresser.

Buckley sniffed at the items she had accumulated in the living room and stared at her with a tilt of his head. He knew something was brewing and he wanted to be a part of it.

She gathered her milking supplies, along with the box and banner, and awkwardly carried everything out to the barn. She opened the van's side door and placed the storage box and banner on a shelf in front of the cattle panel that separated the back of the van from the front. She continued to the barn with her milking supplies.

Once she finished milking, Pearl lured the kids into their night pen with a small bowl of grain. The moms needed to have full udders for the show, so the kids wouldn't be able to nurse for 24 hours.

She began to gather the rest of the items she could load in the evening to save time the next morning. She grabbed the broom and pitchfork and carried them to the van, where she found a space to store them between the driver's seat and the shelves. She pulled out the tack box she had purchased earlier in the year and filled it with the new show collars, leads, clippers for last-minute coat cleanup, hoof trimmers, and brush. She found an extra extension cord, which she might need, depending on where her show pens were located. Satisfied that she had done all the preparation she could for the night, she left the barn, closed the chickens in their coop, and returned to the house.

Chapter 9

Westin's van chugged up the hill to the barn just after sunrise in the morning. *I guess he decided to stay elsewhere last night,* thought Pearl. She had already been out of bed for an hour after tossing and turning all night. She felt distracted and nervous about the show.

Buckley ran ahead to greet him. Pearl met him at the barn, with a cup of coffee in hand—just the way he liked it, with goat milk and two spoons of sugar. He smiled shyly.

"I need to feed the bucks and give the does a little hay before we can load them and the milk stand into my van," She handed him the coffee. "You can put in the bale of alfalfa. I don't have to milk this morning because they have to be full when I show them. If you need something to do, you can give the chickens their scratch and let them out." She laughed.

Once she finished loading the bucks' hay feeder, Pearl returned to the house. She beamed when she saw the chickens outside the coop foraging for insects in the lawn. Now they could load the van.

"I'm ready to get started," she said to Westin. "Let's put Buckley in the house so he doesn't get underfoot. He'll be nervous wondering what's going on."

Westin grabbed Buckley, opened the front door, and placed him on the floor. Pearl retrieved two foldup lawn chairs from the porch and they walked to the barn.

"The milk stand goes into the area behind the seat," she told him. "Do you know how to break it down for transport?" It was a heavy stainless-steel contraption with a flat base for goats to stand on and a stanchion to fit around their necks and keep them in place. The two pieces could be separated and the legs on the base folded up to make it virtually flat.

"It takes up a lot of space, but you can put it in sideways. I'll get the buckets and feed pans, and once you get done with those big things, will you grab that white bucket filled with grain?"

"No problem," said Westin. "I can figure it out." He walked to the milk stand and pulled the stanchion off the base and set it aside. Then he turned the base over and folded the legs in. He carried the heavy apparatus to the van, opened the side door, and set it in on its side, leaning against the seats. He got the stanchion from the barn, and then made another trip to get the bucket of grain.

In between Westin's trips, Pearl had stowed the lawn chairs and stacked and added the buckets, metal bucket hooks, and bowls to the shelves behind the driver's seat, glad to see the bale of alfalfa in the back of the van.

"Thanks for putting the alfalfa in the van. I got a new tarp to protect it from the goats on the way there." She awkwardly reached over the equipment that blocked the way and pulled the new tarp off the shelf and unwrapped it halfway.

"I guess I should have gotten it out first," she laughed. She walked around to the back of the van, opened the double door and made a clumsy attempt to reposition the bale—which paralleled the left side of the van—as she tried to wrap it with the tarp. Without a word, Westin rushed to the back of the van and helped her shift the unwieldy bale to get it covered.

"We just need to add some fresh straw for bedding and we can start loading goats. They don't need any food or water since it's a short drive." Pearl took a deep breath. "Are you ready for the fun part? I'm going to get the goats one by one and lead them out. When I get near, open the gate for me, then shut it and open the back of the van. I'm going to start with the babies. Once I get a goat in the van, you need to block it from getting out and shut the door again. Then we repeat the process."

"That sounds pretty easy," Westin leaned against the van, chuckling.

Pearl got four flakes of wheat straw from the barn and brought them to the back of the van. "Will you break these up and spread them around, then shut one of the back doors while I start bringing the goats out?"

"No problem," said Westin, as he leaned into the van and separated the flakes.

Once in the barn, she had no problem catching the adult does and leading them to the van for loading. Although they weren't used to riding in a vehicle, after two years of handling they were used to being led. Once Pearl got Jinx to the van, she held her by the collar, bent down and grabbed her front feet, which she pulled to the opening.

Westin lifted her back end and Pearl let go of the collar as they shoved Jinx forward. Then he pushed the door shut.

Pearl was panting when it was all over. After she caught her breath, she repeated the process with Kea. She and Westin worked well as a team. That was a huge contrast to working with Pat, who had always seemed to move in the opposite direction, frustrating Pearl no end.

Only two to go—the yearlings, Desi and Lexi. The two junior does appeared panicked as they watched their mothers leave the barn but not return. Pearl realized it would be a rodeo of sorts. She chased Desi around the barn four times before she remembered a better way. She grabbed the big red feed bowl she often used to feed kelp or nutritional yeast, opened the feed can, and grabbed a handful of grain. Then she walked it to the empty stall next to the crying kids, put the bowl on the floor, and walked out while she held the gate open. Desi and Lexi ran into the stall and Pearl shut the gate before they knew what had happened. They were too busy fighting over a minute portion of grain to notice.

Pearl caught her breath, then opened the stall gate. She blocked the exit with her body, grabbed Desi's collar, and dragged her out, latching the gate behind her with her free hand. She alternately walked and dragged Desi—stopping from time to time to avoid choking her—to the van.

"Will you put her in? The little fatty is too much for me to lift. I almost broke my back getting her on the milk stand to clip her. I'll block the door." Pearl gasped from the effort she had expended to get Desi out of the barn to the van.

She opened the van door with the one hand, and held onto the plastic collar with the other, only letting go when Westin picked up the goat around her abdomen and pushed her in.

"One to go!" Pearl was jubilant.

She returned to the stall, grabbed Lexi's collar, and repeated the process. She shut the van door one last time, relieved. She could hear the goats moving around, not about to relax in the small, unfamiliar space.

Back in the barn, Pearl let the kids out of their pen from the night before. They zoomed out, crying and searching in desperation for their moms—to no avail. One by one they drifted over to the hay feeder and began to eat.

Pearl returned to the back of the van, where Westin still stood. "I need to change into my show whites before we leave. I figured they would be filthy by the time we got the goats loaded if I put them on first. I also have to give Buckley a marrow bone since he has to be alone at home all day. Then we can get on the road," she said.

"That sounds like a plan," said Westin.

They arrived at the fairgrounds 45 minutes later, after an uneventful trip.

Pearl walked into the livestock barn serenaded by the screams of Nubians and Nigerians—the loudest breeds. She surveyed the huge metal livestock barn, waved to a few people who were unloading their goats, and found her assigned pens. She spread the wood shavings supplied by the fairgrounds in two pens. The third would serve as a supply and tack area as well as a place for Pearl and Westin to hang out.

Eager to get out of their crowded quarters, the goats unloaded easily, even the yearlings. Pearl and Westin removed the alfalfa and other items and relocated them in the tack pen.

"I'm going to get this area organized and get the goats some alfalfa. Will you go find the water faucet and fill a bucket for each stall?"

"No problem." He picked up the buckets and three bucket hooks.

She cut the strings on the alfalfa bale, stuffed the feed bags, and hung one in each stall. The goats acted as if they were starved, grabbing mouthfuls of alfalfa. Since grass hay was their main diet and they usually got alfalfa only in the evenings, this was a treat. Westin had already assembled the milk stand in one corner in the back of the tack stall.

After he hung a water bucket in each goat stall, Westin came into the tack stall and flopped into one of the chairs.

"I'm going to move the van out to the parking lot now," said Pearl. "I'll put my sign up when I get back." She turned and strode out of the livestock barn.

She walked to the van, ebullient that things were going so smoothly. She couldn't believe her luck with Westin arriving at her house when he did. She wished Pat weren't dead, but at least she wasn't left on her own.

Pearl vowed that she would have a good time at the goat show, a much-needed distraction from ruminating on who might have murdered her shed boy. And she hoped her goats would win some ribbons, too.

Chapter 10

Pearl entered the livestock barn. She took a deep breath through her nose; she loved the smell of hay, goat manure, and goats. It reminded her of childhood vacations to visit relatives on farms in Nebraska. While Ruby had gone overboard to hide her roots, Pearl instead embraced them. She had always loved animals.

She had about an hour before the show started. As she approached her pens, she noticed a heavy-set woman sitting in her chair, engaged in conversation with Westin. It was Zora Vega. Pearl rolled her eyes and then took a deep breath to steel herself. She was unprepared to deal with the off-putting woman when she heard, "Pearl! You made it. How many goats did you bring?"

She pointed to her pens. "Right there; four. Two does in milk and two dry juniors. I couldn't bring the kids because I had no way to separate them on the way here. How about you?"

"I brought six seniors, four dry yearlings, and 10 doelings. I think I have at least one in each age group," she said, self-importantly. Pearl sighed. Whenever she had a conversation with Zora, she felt bad afterward. *Zora pretends to be nice but actually thinks she is superior. When I have a few years of goat breeding under my belt, I'll be a mentor to newbies, not someone who acts better than others.*

"Oh, look, Sarah's here!" said Pearl, glad for the distraction. A tall, dark-haired woman with intense brown eyes made her way down the aisle with a bucket in each hand to get water for her goats. She smiled when she saw Pearl and walked faster.

Sarah was one of the first goat people Pearl had met when she moved to Middle Pass. Sarah was a cheerleader for all new goat owners and a founder of the Middle Pass Goat Club (MPGC). She was always willing to answer questions, consult on a problem, or just encourage a new goat owner to register and show their goats. She was also a nurse, something she and Pearl had in common.

Sarah paused in front of Pearl. "I'm glad you made it!" she said enthusiastically. She glanced at Zora. "Hi, Zora.

"I'd stop and talk," she said to Pearl, "but I have to get my goat pens ready before the show starts. I'm co-secretary, so I have to record all the placings and make sure the paperwork for the wins is accurate. I'm in charge of paperwork for the larger breeds, since I'll be showing my Nigerians later."

"I'll let you go then," said Pearl, disappointed to be forced to face Zora again, without another knowledgeable person to contradict some of the crazy things she said. "Good luck in the show!"

"Good luck to you, too, Pearl," said Sarah brightly. "I know you'll do well."

Pearl turned back to Westin and Zora. She couldn't tell from his face whether he was annoyed by Zora or not.

"Don't you have something you need to do?" she asked Zora. Hopefully she would get the hint and move on.

"Oh, we have until after lunch," said Zora. "The standard breeds go first and they take all morning. I'm free until after lunch when we show Nigerian kids. They probably won't get to the dry yearlings until 2:00 this afternoon so you have plenty of time.

"A different subject, but did you guys find out any more about who killed Pat?" Zora turned and addressed Westin. Pearl cringed. "My brother's son's wife's brother heard something about Ward Fowler and Pat getting into it last month. You know, he's the guy who owns the Ace Hardware in town. They. …

"I think you mean your nephew's brother-in-law, Zora," Pearl said condescendingly. "Please! Can we not talk about a dead man at the goat show? I thought we came here to focus on goats and forget about depressing events going on in the world."

Zora looked shocked, as she turned her gaze from Westin to Pearl to Westin again. "Well, sorry. I thought you might care since it was your handyman who got killed," she said in a snotty voice.

"Okay. I'm going to see what the setup looks like and see who else is here from the goat club. I'll talk to you later." Pearl turned and headed down the aisle, relieved to be away from Zora.

The goat show was an overall success, despite Pearl's nervousness about being inexperienced. The yearlings didn't cooperate—stopping mid-walk and trying to lie down when they were supposed to be standing still—but despite Desi's refusal to be posed, she must have had something going for her because she took first place in her junior class.

Pearl was glad she hadn't brought her doelings after she watched the kids that had been entered in the show strain on their leads, jump sideways, stop to pee, and overall refuse to work together with their owners.

When two-year-olds were being shown, Jinx trotted around the ring like she had been showing all her life. Pearl remembered to keep her eyes on the judge at all times, but she hadn't quite mastered turning to face her when they rounded a corner or setting her doe up properly so her back looked flat. In the end it hadn't mattered. The judge could tell a good quality goat when she saw one and Jinx took first place in her class, as well as Best Udder. Zora was muttering under her breath as the judge explained why she had placed each of the goats where she did.

Kea came in third place. She didn't have the conformation Jinx did, but it also might have been because Westin showed her. Pearl hadn't considered that she would have to show both her two-year-olds at the same time, and would need some help. *Thank goodness she had Westin.* She couldn't imagine what nightmare it would have been if Pat had been there. He always worried that he would hurt the goats and allowed them to run roughshod over him.

Pearl was thrilled to be able to talk goats with Sarah and other club members other than Zora throughout the day. Shortly before noon, Jane had arrived, with Ruby and Scheherazade not far behind, giving them a chance to have lunch together before Pearl's goats were scheduled to be shown. They ordered vegetarian Yumm bowls from Café Yumm and had them delivered.

Pearl had been surprised at how glad she was to see her family. Even though Ruby disapproved of her chosen path, at least she was willing to act supportive from time to time. Pearl had her goat friends and Jane, but that wasn't the same as family. She proudly introduced Westin to them as her new helper.

When Pearl and Ruby got up to go to the restroom before their lunch arrived, Jane had turned to Westin. "I wanted to let you know how much I appreciated your help with the garden the day before the tour. I don't know if you heard, but I got grand prize again."

Pearl hesitated, but then continued on. She hadn't been aware that Westin had done work for Jane. *It's good that he has other work,* she thought. *It's not my business what he does in his free time.*

"You have no idea how much it means to me that you and Scheherazade decided to come to the show. I love having you here," Pearl said to Ruby as they were washing their hands afterward.

"We didn't have anything else to do today. It's certainly different than what we normally do on the weekend. Thanks for inviting us." Ruby seemed genuine, a rare but welcomed change from her normal judgmental attitude. But, of course, she couldn't stop there.

"Who is this Westin, anyway? Scheherazade said he was just some random homeless guy who lives in his van. How well do you know him?" Ruby looked at Pearl intently.

Pearl felt a sick sensation in her stomach. *Why can't she leave well enough alone?* "I've known him for about a year now and he's a perfectly nice guy. Don't be such a classist. Anyway, he helped me get the goats here and he's going to help me show them, too. When we get back, you and Scheherazade need to go with Jane and find a seat before the next show starts. And please try to be supportive!"

Ruby looked at Pearl, seemingly oblivious. "I am being supportive; I'm here, aren't I?"

Pearl took a deep breath and willed herself to focus on what she came to the show for as they walked back to join the others.

Chapter 11

The first thing to enter her mind when she awoke in the morning was the goat show the day before. Pearl was thrilled that Jinx had won first place in the two-year-old category and Desi had won first place as a dry yearling! She had hoped for Best of Breed for Jinx, but at least she had won Best Udder. It was quite a coup for her first goat show.

Her dream of raising prize-winning dairy goats was turning out just like she had planned, other than losing Pat. She was still a little miffed that Ruby and Scheherazade had been so judgmental but at least they showed up. And Jane. Maybe she and Jane would be friends, after all. Since she had moved out to Middle Pass, her city friends had dropped off, one by one. They thought the drive was too far but thought nothing of Pearl's drive into town. She hadn't realized it before, but she could use a close friend in her new-found hometown.

Pearl was still on Cloud Nine when she got back from doing her morning chores. She poured her second cup of coffee and took a seat at the dining room table. She took a sip just as Buckley let out a yip followed by several barks. He must have been asleep. She heard a knock on the door. Through the window she saw Dan's sheriff hat.

"Come in," said Pearl. She opened the door wide. "Would you like some coffee or tea?"

The sheriff pulled out a chair, took off his hat, and sat at the table. Buckley read this move as a sign to leap onto his lap. He grinned. "I don't have time to stick around. I'm on duty right now but wanted to keep in touch with you about Pat's death. We're still waiting for the toxicology results. They can take up to six weeks, although we hope to get them within a month. It depends on the lab's workload.

"We do know that Pat ate at the café and went to the Pub from there. That would explain the alcohol. But we don't know what happened between the time he left the Pub and his death."

Pearl nodded her head and confessed, "Yes, I talked to Dave myself and he told me Pat had insisted on a drink after getting the money from his check. But he left after that and didn't come back. If that's true, it raises the question of why his blood alcohol was as high as it was."

The sheriff shook his head in disapproval. "Pearl, I told you to stay out of this and let law enforcement handle it. There are some rough characters who frequent the Pub."

"Oh, don't worry. I went during the day. I'll be fine." *It was kind of sweet that he was worried about her.*

The sheriff put Buckley down on the floor and stood. "You really need to leave the investigation to the police. So far, we have no reason to believe any foul play occurred."

"I just wanted to find out what Pat was doing that day. No harm in that, is there?" Pearl said, trying to appear innocent.

"Please stay out of it. Things are moving slowly, but you have to come to terms with Pat's uncharacteristic drinking and then death. If there's anything to find, we'll do it."

"Okay, Dan. I won't cause any trouble. Thanks for the update. I appreciate it." She held the door open for him. "Drive safely."

So Pat had definitely been at the café. Pearl would have to take a little trip down there to find out what Vern and Lorena knew, if anything. Besides, they had good burgers. She sat at the dining room table deep in thought when Buckley began his barking routine. A knock rattled the front door.

It was Westin. He had spent the night in his van in the driveway by the shed. He always slept late, so Pearl wasn't surprised that it was 11:00 am.

She opened the door. "You finally decided to get up?"

He rubbed his eyes, still half asleep.

"You look like you could use some coffee. Do you need to take a shower first? I planned to go to the Armadillo Café, so you can come with me after you get showered if you want."

"That sounds good. I'll go get some clean clothes and my towel."

Pearl didn't say anything about him working for Jane. After all, she had no claim on how he spent his time. Still, she was bothered that he had never mentioned it. *How many other secrets did he have?*

They sat in the worn middle stools at the Armadillo Café's laminate counter. The odor of grease from the deep fryer permeated the air in the small building, despite the recent paint job.

Pearl knew the café had gone through quite a few different hands over the years. Many people dreamed of running a little restaurant out in the country, but so far they had all found that with this one, financial success was unreachable. The latest owners were Vern and Lorena Davis, who had seen the For Sale sign as they drove through the area on vacation from Texas two years earlier.

Vern was one of only two black men in Middle Pass. He was dark-skinned and of average height and average weight. Lorena was white and chunky, on a five-foot frame. She had bleach-damaged blonde hair and wore jewelry mostly in turquoise and armadillo motifs.

Like all the prior owners, they used the café as an opportunity to showcase a quirky theme—in this case, armadillos. A neon armadillo-shaped sign hung over the front of the building. Lorena had a collection of every kind of armadillo collectible imaginable, from glass to ceramic to metal to plushies. They were displayed on shelves that lined the café walls. She had also sewed custom curtains for the front windows out of tan fabric with gray armadillos. Different armadillo salt-and-pepper shakers occupied each table. Mismatched armadillo-themed mugs held the bottomless coffee that was the café's loss leader.

The café served breakfast all day, as well as burgers, soups, salads, and a different dinner special each day—some with armadillo-themed names. Vern and Lorena hired a few local young people to work part-time in the café during the weekends, but they did the bulk of the work themselves. They were open six days a week and took Monday off to go into town to buy supplies for the coming week. It was a labor of love—but one guaranteed to burn them out.

Pearl knew most of the regulars as well as the staff, even though she ate there only once a month or so.

"Welcome, y'all!" said Vern.

"You're Westin, right?" He smiled at Westin, who nodded. Vern could remember a person's name even after just one meeting. His friendly personality and down-home cooking brought customers from as far as Eugene and Florence.

Lorena appeared from the back of the café. She wore an apron featuring a purple and green armadillo and sported armadillo earrings. She nodded in recognition at Pearl and handed them menus.

"How are you two doing?" asked Pearl.

"We're great," said Lorena. "How are the goats?"

"The goats are doing fine. Westin just helped me with a goat show yesterday. This was my first year showing them. I'm pretty excited about the ribbons my goats won."

"Coffee?" asked Lorena.

Westin nodded enthusiastically. "Yes, please," said Pearl. She opened her menu and browsed it for a moment.

She scanned the restaurant. There were the usual locals—Larry, Helen, and Shirley at the end of the counter, and a few families at the tables in the other section of the building. She smiled and waved at the locals, then returned to her menu.

"I'm buying." Westin beamed.

Pearl looked up, surprised. He usually didn't have much money. She bit her tongue. She wouldn't embarrass him by questioning his offer. "Thanks, Westin. That's generous."

They both ordered the cheese "armadillo burger." Pearl rarely ate beef at a restaurant, but she knew the meat at the Armadillo was pasture-raised and local, which, to her, made it acceptable.

While they ate, the café gradually emptied of customers. Only Pearl, Westin, and Helen remained. A fixture in town, Helen sported dyed red hair and glasses and she had a penchant for gossip. She had lived alone since her husband died the year before. She took advantage of the bottomless coffee, often staying for hours.

Pearl leaned over the counter and peered into the kitchen. "Hey, Vern. Do you have a minute to talk?"

He glanced at Lorena, who nodded. "Okay, I have nothing cooking right now, but if I get another order, I'll have to cut it short."

He put a spatula down next to the grill and walked out to the counter. He was an unimposing, soft-spoken man of few words. He wore an armadillo apron identical to Lorena's.

110

Lorena walked out the back door of the kitchen to the dining room and took the opportunity to refill salt and pepper shakers and ketchup bottles on the tables there.

"I suppose you guys heard about Pat." Pearl pushed her empty plate toward the front of the counter and picked up her ice water.

"Yeah." Vern furrowed his brow. "To be honest, I can't say I'm sorry he's gone. That guy makes a wasp look cuddly."

"Vern, don't speak ill of the dead," Lorena chided from across the room. She was working but was listening to every word.

"Well, he *was* a jerk…." retorted Vern.

"Did you see him that day? Was he here? I know he ate here pretty often since he didn't have a place to cook on my farm."

"Oh, yeah, he was here that afternoon. His usual complaining self. Nothing out of the normal. He seemed excited about something he had gotten in the mail, but we don't talk more than we have to, so I have no idea what it was about." Vern shook his head and wiped his hands on his apron.

"I'm just trying to figure out what he did that day, who he talked to, what happened. The sheriff says it was an accident—he fell and hit his head—but it just seems strange to me. His blood alcohol also showed that he had been drinking, but he doesn't normally drink. He didn't he have a beer or anything here, did he?"

111

"No. He didn't buy any beer or wine from us. I haven't seen him drink since I met him. I'm sorry I can't offer much help but, like I said, he acted like a jerk, as usual. That man could start a fight in an empty building." Vern, averse to the slightest hint of conflict, mumbled something else, then returned to the kitchen.

Lorena went into the kitchen from the dining room and came out behind the counter to face Pearl. "Don't mind him," she whispered. "He and Pat never saw eye to eye. Vern can't handle argumentative people, so he usually just walks away. He's had to deal with racism his whole life and, honestly, it isn't any better in Oregon than it is in Texas. He worked hard for everything he has, and he expects people to be grateful for what they have, too."

Pearl had noticed Helen looking over from time to time as she thumbed through the newspaper and drank her coffee. She seemed to be eavesdropping on their conversation, but she said nothing. Pearl was going to say something to her, but Helen suddenly left her payment with the check on the counter and walked out the front door.

"How late are you open?" Pearl finished her water and put the glass back on the counter.

"We're closed on Mondays, but we're open until 8:00 every other night but Sunday and then cleanup takes another couple of hours. We leave at 6:00 pm on Sundays."

"That's a long day," Pearl shook her head commiserating. "Do you both work until closing each day? How do you do it?"

Westin watched pensively, not adding to the conversation.

"Yes. It's a lot of work, but this is our dream and we love doing it. Sometimes one of us takes Tuesday morning to go into town to get more supplies." Lorena tallied the check for Westin and Pearl and set it in front of his empty plate.

🏠

"Well, that wasn't very helpful," Pearl said to Westin, as they got into the van. "But the lunch was delicious, so thank you for treating."

"Pearl, I think you just need to accept the fact that Pat fell down accidentally," said Westin. "No one could have done anything about it since it was after dark and he was out in the woods."

Pearl turned to him. "I guess you're right. Can we stop by the store on the way home? I just have to run in and get some ice cream. I like to have it in the freezer for when I get a craving."

"No, problem. I don't need anything so I'm just going to wait in the car."

Westin pulled into the parking lot. Pearl got out of the car and walked toward the market. As she approached the door, it swung open and Helen came out carrying a small paper bag. She wore a ratty corduroy coat and tan wool cap covered most of her crimson hair. Pearl almost didn't recognize her with the hat on.

Helen grabbed Pearl by the arm. She looked around, then spoke. "Vern and Lorena didn't tell you about what happened with Pat a few weeks ago. I think you should know."

Pearl's eyes grew wide. "What do you mean?"

"Pat had seemed in a good mood when he got to the Armadillo that day, but after he ordered he started acting crazy. He got all riled up and was shouting about how bad the food was there and how Vern needed to learn how to cook and his wife was a lousy waitress. He just got louder and louder, until Vern told him to get out." She gestured excitedly.

"I heard him in the kitchen saying, 'I want to kill that jerk!' Pat refused to leave and I was honestly surprised that Lorena didn't say anything. The only time Pat shut up was when he was eating. Then when he was done, he started in again and by the time he left he had basically cleared out the café. No one wanted to be there with him. He scared a lot of people. I wasn't scared because I know him and I know how he can be. But it wasn't a pretty sight. Vern looked like he was going to have a stroke. He was clenching his fists and his eyes were about to pop out of his head. I believe he would have hit Pat if Lorena hadn't intervened. And this wasn't the first time they had such a serious altercation." Helen stopped to catch her breath.

She continued, "Lorena is so nice. She didn't want to ban him. Vern didn't know what to do. Pat was so hot and

114

cold. They kept hoping for the nice Pat and then when the crazy Pat came out, they didn't know how to react. Vern was furious. I just thought you should be aware. I can't figure out why they didn't tell you how bad it was. After all, he's dead, so he can't do anything about it now."

Pearl was stunned. This was the first she had heard of this. On the rare occasion when she had been in the café with Pat, he was his usual prickly self, but not out of the bounds of socially acceptable. *What were the Davises hiding?*

She thanked Helen and returned to the van, having forgotten her craving for ice cream.

"What was that all about? She seemed pretty excited about something." Westin looked puzzled.

"She said Vern had been downplaying his last encounter with Pat at the café. She told me he had actually been really furious because Pat gave him a hard time about the food and refused to leave. She claimed that Vern and Pat had nearly come to blows and Vern had threatened to kill Pat. She said she had never seen Vern so mad before." Pearl bit her lip.

"He did have a way of pushing people to the edge at times," said Westin. "Where's your ice cream?"

"Helen got me upset, even if she is a gossip. I forgot I went to get ice cream. I don't want any now. Something isn't right. Still, despite what she said, it doesn't seem like Vern would have had the opportunity to kill Pat, since he apparently works all the time. Even if I go back in the café and ask him where he was later that night, I wouldn't expect either him or Lorena to tell me if he had left the café."

She shook her head. "It seems like every time I learn something new, there's more I need to find out."

"Come on, Pearl. The sheriff said it was an accident, and you need to let it go. If all the people Pat offended are murder suspects, you'll have to interview the whole town and then some." He laughed.

Pearl got quiet, worried.

Chapter 12

After Westin left, Pearl decided to make a call to Deadwood and schedule a meeting with Joe since he had been the last known person to see Pat and may have had a motive to steal his money.

She got the post-it note from the whiteboard and sat in the living room. She dialed the number she assumed was for Joe's mother. She was about to hang up after the fifth ring when a woman answered.

"Hi, my name is Pearl Kelly. May I speak to Joe?"

"He isn't here right now. I expect him to be home around 4:00. He's planning to pick up his son at 4:30 today from the afterschool program and then they'll come back here for dinner. Are you a friend of his?"

"No; I'm calling about Pat Steinberg. Did you hear about his death?"

"Oh, yes, Joe told me. I have no idea who the man was, though. I don't think he and Joe were friends; it was just someone he knew from the bar. Why do you need to talk to Joe?" asked Mrs. Martinez.

"He may have been one of the last people to see Pat alive, so I wanted to talk to him about what he saw. Do you think I could come out and talk to him tonight?" Pearl bit her bottom lip.

"Sure; I'd think he'd want to help if he could," she replied. "We should be done with dinner at 6:00, so why don't you plan to come out then. We aren't going anywhere. Just watching TV. I hope he doesn't mind me inviting you without checking first."

"Oh, don't worry, Mrs. Martinez. I just need to clarify some things. I really appreciate your help." Pearl let out a sigh of relief.

"I might bring a friend with me," she said. She would go to Jane's and see if Jane would agree to go with her. And if there were any danger—which she thought unlikely—it would be safety in numbers. "See you in a few hours."

Pearl slipped into a jacket and opened the front door to black clouds and a torrent of rain. She grabbed Buckley and ran to the Subaru, dodging raindrops. She felt nervous about going to a stranger's house, but she had to get an idea of who he was and whether he might be a likely suspect. He had motive, after all. Pat had owed him money and recently came into a lot of it. She would feel a little safer with Jane along.

"I'm so glad you came to the goat show," said Pearl. She settled Buckley on her lap on Jane's floral couch. "It helps to have the moral support."

"Oh, you're welcome. I'm pretty busy with my gardening, but I don't have many other outside interests and it gave me an opportunity to get out with other people and do something new." Jane rocked in the chair facing Pearl. "It was great to see Westin again and meet your sister and niece, too."

"I overheard you thanking Westin for help with your garden. I didn't realize you already knew him and he'd done work for you. He's so much help. Maybe he can lend a hand with your end-of-the-season work, too."

"Yes, Pat introduced me to him. I ran into them at the café one day and Pat suggested that he could help with some of the heavier lifting. He's a real gem. I don't know how I would have gotten everything ready for the Garden Club Tour without him." Jane smoothed her pant leg.

Pearl nervously petted her little dog. "You know I'm trying to find out what happened to Pat. And with the goat show behind me, I've started working on the investigation again. Westin took me out to lunch at the Armadillo today and I had a chance to talk to Vern and Lorena since Pat ate there often.

"According to what they told me, Pat ate a meal in the afternoon and then he left. They claimed he was his usual difficult self, but he didn't drink any alcohol there and nothing else was out of the ordinary. I found it helpful, but not helpful, because it only told me what he didn't do.

"The weird part is what happened after we left the café. Do you know Helen, who hangs out at the counter there all the time?"

Jane nodded. "Older lady, kind of a busybody? Red-headed?"

"She's the one," said Pearl. "Well, I walked over to the store to get some ice cream after we had lunch and before I could even go into the store, she came out the door and told me a story about Vern and Pat getting into it a few weeks ago. She said Vern was so angry that he had to be stopped from attacking Pat.

"So while that gives him a motive for killing Pat, according to Lorena they never leave the café until 10 pm at night, except for Sundays when they close earlier and Monday, when they are closed. How well do you know them, Jane?"

"I wouldn't say we're good friends," said Jane, "but I know them fairly well since they're active in the garden club. That is, Lorena is active. She has a real nice garden, but she doesn't enter it in the annual tour yet. I think Vern just goes along with her interests and they want to be a part of the community in general."

"What's your impression of them?" asked Pearl.

"They seem like a nice, quiet couple. Lorena's more outgoing than Vern. She came over last month to help me fold and address brochures for the Garden Club Tour. She's quite sensitive to any hint of racism, and protective of Vern, probably because of what they experienced as a couple in Texas. According to Lorena, she comes from a family of bigots and she's estranged from them now. She said she tried to get them to accept Vern, but she eventually had to pull away—and move far away—to escape from the microagressions and rude comments. It's not easy being a mixed-race couple, you know." Jane sat back in her chair.

"I usually go to the café once a week or so, just to get out. They've always been friendly with me. I just can't imagine mild-mannered Vern being mad enough to follow Pat and hurt him that night. But at least you shed some light on what happened on Pat's last day, for what it's worth." Jane sighed deeply.

"You're probably right. But do you think Pat was racist? I'm not aware of anything that would make me think he was a bigot." Pearl scratched her head.

"No, I agree with you, Pearl. I wouldn't have a relationship with someone who showed signs of being a racist. Between you and me, I think that because of their past experiences, Lorena is quick to jump to racism when people cause conflict with them." Jane stared intently at Pearl.

Pearl nodded. "On another note, I finally connected with Joe Martinez—well, his mother anyway—and I'm going out to his place in Deadwood at 6:00 tonight. Would you be willing to go with me? You've met him, so I thought maybe it would be less awkward with both of us there. What do you think?"

Jane raised her eyebrows, then gazed toward the ceiling in thought. "As far as we know, he was the last person to see Pat, right? Unless Dave made that up. I don't totally trust what he says. From what I could tell, Joe is a good guy, though. He just has an alcohol problem. I guess it couldn't hurt anything. Sure. I'll go."

"Thank you!" said Pearl, relieved. "We need to leave around 5:15 to get there at 6:00. I'm going to go back and do

121

my chores so we don't have to hurry to get back home right away. I'll probably have a bite to eat before we go, too."

Pearl stood to go. "I'll pick you up at 5:15."

Joe Martinez and his mother lived in a small but tidy log house. Pearl and Jane wiped their wet feet on the little carpet square in front of the door. "Should we take our shoes off?" asked Pearl.

"Oh, no. You're fine," said Mrs. Martinez. "I can take your coats." They took off their coats and gave them to her to hang up. They walked into the living area to a cozy scene: wood stove blazing with a warm fire, a long couch with colorful throw pillows and crocheted afghans, matching coffee table and end tables, and several chairs. A large picture of the Virgin Mary had a place of honor on one wall and a crucifix on another. Pearl was impressed that no TV dominated the room, like in so many homes these days.

"I hope we aren't interrupting anything," said Pearl. "I'm Pearl Kelly and I think you've met Jane Wilson, right?"

"Jane and I have seen each other at the Pub, I think. My son is watching TV in the other room. Mom, will you go hang out with him? Would either of you like a beer?" Joe held up a Corona beer.

"No, not me," said Pearl. "Maybe a glass of water. Jane?"

"Sure, I'll have a beer," said Jane.

Mrs. Martinez left the room. After they got settled with their drinks, Pearl began, "I'm sure you were aware that Pat Steinberg, my hired hand, was killed a few weeks ago. When I talked to Dave Miller at the Pub, he said you had left the Pub at the same time as Pat. So you were one of the last people to see him."

Joe's face reddened. He reclined and took a large gulp of beer. "Am I a suspect?"

"Oh, no," Pearl shook her head. "I'm not with law enforcement; I'm just a private citizen. He was a friend of ours" —she looked at Jane— "and we're trying to piece things together. The police say it was an accident. But he had a lot of money and it seems to be missing, so we're sort of retracing his steps."

"Well, it's interesting you mention that about the money. He owed me a few hundred dollars and, you're right, I did leave at the same time as Pat. I followed him out the door because I wanted to ask for repayment while he was flush. I only found out about it because he was kind of loud and bragging about his inheritance. I'd never seen him drinking before and he was acting a little unusual.

"Anyway, I followed him out of the Pub and straight out asked him if he would pay me back so I could get my son the bicycle he wanted. He reached in his pocket, pulled out a wad and repaid me right there."

"How did he look and act otherwise?" asked Jane. Pearl gave an approving nod, glad she had brought her along. They could make a good team.

"He actually looked a little queasy. His color wasn't too good. He said he was going home."

"What happened then?" asked Pearl.

"When I was walking to my truck, he started walking south. As I got into my truck, I saw a dark blue van pull up beside him and he stopped and they were talking. The driver was a younger guy. As I pulled onto the highway, Pat was getting into the passenger side of the van."

Pearl and Jane looked at each other. The only person in town they knew who drove a dark blue van was Westin. But he had told Pearl he was at the coast that night.

"Did you recognize the person in the van, or the kind of van?" asked Pearl.

"No," said Joe. "He stood on the side of the van farthest from me, so all I could tell was that the guy wasn't old. He had dark hair. I don't spend a lot of time in Middle Pass, either, and it wasn't anyone I knew from the Pub. As to the make of the van, I'm not a big car person. I can't tell the difference between a Plymouth or a Ford."

"Has the sheriff talked to you about this?" Pearl took a drink of water.

"No," said Joe. "I try to keep a low profile. I thought I had heard it was an accident. If that's the case, why would they even spend the time interviewing me?"

"We aren't so sure it *was* an accident. And the rest of the money he had has gone missing. Do you remember where you went after you left the Pub?" asked Jane.

"I came straight home. I usually stop at the Pub after work and have a few beers, then head home. I got here at 6:30, as far as I remember."

"Is there anything else you can think of that might be helpful?" asked Pearl.

Joe shook his head, then finished his beer and placed the empty bottle on the table next to him.

Pearl turned to Jane, who shrugged, drank the last of her beer, then stood and walked to the kitchen with the empty bottle. Joe and Pearl followed her lead.

"Thanks for your help. And it was nice to meet you, Joe, despite these circumstances. Tell your mom thank you." Pearl shook his hand.

Jane came back from the kitchen. "Where are our coats?" she asked.

Joe walked to the front hall closet, opened it, and threw their coats over his arm. "Here you are, ladies. I hope you have a safe drive home. Let me know if I can help in any way."

Chapter 13

Their car doors were barely shut before both Jane and Pearl started to talk at the same time.

"Who else in town has a dark blue van?" asked Pearl. She turned on the ignition.

"I have no idea," Jane exclaimed. "Did you already talk to Westin about that night?"

"No," said Pearl. She put the seat warmers on low.

"I saw him the following morning and told him about finding Pat's body. I'm sure he told me he had only gotten back from the coast that morning. I wonder why he would lie? I consider myself a good judge of character, so how could I have gotten this so wrong? In fact, I didn't even know he had done work for you until I overheard you thanking him for moving plants before the Garden Tour. When did you last see him before we found Pat?"

Pearl turned on the lights, backed out of the driveway, and headed east down the highway for home. The two women were silent for a few minutes, as their thoughts churned.

"I hadn't seen him since the day he helped me with plants. It was the day before the tour. He did all the heavy lifting, getting things from the greenhouse, moving heavy pots and statues. I agree with you on his character. I had pegged him as an honest guy. Maybe you misunderstood what he said." Jane looked over at Pearl, eyebrows raised.

Pearl bristled. "I know what I heard. Why would he try to mislead me? I hope he stops by tomorrow so I can talk to him. I have no way to reach him right now. I need to get this resolved. I've been cleaning Pat's shed and had planned to offer it to Westin. It's kind of sudden, but I hoped that having a shed to stay in, instead of a van, would be enough incentive to get him to stay through the winter and help out. And if it worked out, he could stay even longer. He would be a big help to both of us." She chewed on her lip.

"I'm sure he'll have a logical explanation … if it was even him," said Jane. "I'm sure he isn't the only one in the county with a dark blue van."

Pearl felt annoyed. She hoped the same thing, but for some reason Jane saying it got on her nerves. She turned on the classical music station to fill the void and keep Jane from talking. They drove home the rest of the way in silence. Pearl needed to think.

Pearl woke up the next morning feeling less than refreshed. She had a sick feeling in her stomach when she thought about what they had learned the night before. But Buckley didn't have time for such introspection. He insisted that they begin the daily routine by stretching and rolling around on the bed until Pearl couldn't lie there any longer.

After coffee and chores, Pearl would finish cleaning the shed so if Westin had a good explanation, she could offer it to him for the winter.

"C'mon, Buckley," she said to the little white puffball, even though he never needed to be encouraged to stick to her like Velcro. She awkwardly carried a broom and dustpan, a dust rag, a mop, a sponge, a plastic trash bag, and a bucket of hot detergent water to the shed. She would get all of Pat's belongings out and scrub it well. She wouldn't put on clean bedding until she got a new shed boy.

Pearl got the cardboard box she had left on the previous visit and gathered paperwork, soda cans, books, the contents of the nightstand drawer, and other items to be sorted, and put them into the box. Since she had disposed of all the food, clothing, and trash, there wasn't much more to remove. Buckley perched quietly on the bare mattress and watched her work.

Pearl methodically dusted and cleaned the microwave and mini fridge, then the tabletops and the walls. She swept the dust, hay, and other debris from the floor out the front door. It didn't appear that Pat had cleaned it since he moved in. She washed the walls and hadn't even begun mopping the floor, yet the mop water already looked muddy. Pearl picked up the bucket and started out the front door to go back to the house to replace it with clean water for the floor when she saw the sheriff's vehicle approaching.

The sheriff parked his car and stepped out the door and waved to Pearl. Buckley barked once and scurried over to him.

"Come on in. I was just cleaning the shed. I still need to finish mopping, but I could stand to take a break," she yelled to him.

They converged at the front porch, with Dan already holding Buckley. Pearl led the way into the house, took her bucket into the laundry room and dumped the fouled water into the sink, then set the empty bucket on top of the washing machine. When she came out, the sheriff had already pulled out one of the wooden chairs and sat at the dining room table.

"Are you here for milk or crime?" Pearl eyed him warily. "Or just to see your best friend?" She saw Buckley settled on Dan's lap and chuckled.

"All three! Darn, I left the jar in the car." He snapped his fingers as he spoke. "I'll get you the empty jar when I take the fresh milk out to the cooler."

"Well, you've accomplished number three. I'll get you the milk when you're ready to leave. So what's going on with the case? I have some questions about it for you, too. Like, are you even doing any investigation?" Pearl liked Dan, but she still wondered whether the investigation was getting short shrift because Pat was a nobody.

"You know I can't share all the information with you, Pearl." Dan pursed his lips and frowned.

"You especially can't share something if you don't know it," she complained. "For instance, who were the last people to see Pat that night? I know for a fact you haven't interviewed Joe Martinez."

"At this point, like I told you before, the death is considered accidental. So it wouldn't matter who had last seen him."

Pearl let out a sigh. "It matters to me. It matters to Jane. It matters to the people who cared about him. We want to find out what led to his death. And what about his inheritance? Someone had to have taken it. Money doesn't just disappear."

The sheriff put a warm hand on Pearl's shoulder. "Come on, Pearl. You know it takes time to solve these cases. I did get some further information from the medical examiner, but I'm not sure it means anything or is helpful at all. The medical examiner reported that he found some partially digested chicken, as well as a brown woody substance, which he couldn't identify, in the stomach contents." He watched Pearl's eyes widen as he delivered the news. "That's about it. The cause of death is still undetermined until the autopsy is completed, although we know he had a skull fracture."

"So what now? Will you interview anyone else? You don't need to bother with Joe Martinez because Jane and I were at his house last night. Dave said Joe was the last one to see Pat. We learned something else interesting; the actual last person to see him was a guy driving a dark blue van." Buckley watched Pearl as her voice got louder.

131

The sheriff looked pensive. After a minute, he fixed his gaze on Pearl. "Doesn't your friend Westin, who I met the other day, drive a dark blue van?"

Pearl found herself tearing up. "I haven't been able to get ahold of him since Joe told us Pat had gotten in the van with this guy that night. I hope it wasn't him, because he had told me he didn't get back from the coast until the morning I found Pat. And I was just starting to depend on him to help me around the farm."

Dan patted Pearl's hand. "Well, there are plenty of dark blue vans in Lane County. Did Joe identify Westin as the driver?"

"No, he couldn't see the driver well enough. I'm going to talk to Westin about it the next time I see him. But like I said, I don't think it was him." She pulled a tissue from her pocket and dabbed at her eyes. She didn't want to cry in front of Dan.

"Now about that milk...." said the sheriff, eager to change the subject. He stood and put Buckley on the floor. "Let me go out and get my clean jar while you get the milk." He opened the door and took a step onto the porch while he held Buckley in with his other foot, then let the screen door close behind him.

Pearl opened the refrigerator and found the freshest milk for him. She wished Westin would come back soon. *Could Pat's stomach contents provide any clue as to how he died?* She hadn't thought to ask the Davises what Pat had eaten that day, although she now suspected it was probably chicken in some form.

Chapter 14

With her investigation into Pat's whereabouts at a lull, Pearl needed something else to engage her attention. She didn't feel like reading and the black clouds that had let loose that morning made it impossible to go outside for a walk with the goats, who disliked rain even more than Pearl did.

She remembered what Jane had told her about someone stealing the seeds on her table during the Garden Club Tour. *Maybe she should try to solve that mystery.*

Pearl made a cup of tea and planted herself in the rocking chair, opened her laptop, and googled "pong pong seeds." A number of ads for ordering them from e-Bay popped up. She learned that the large seeds were used to make knickknacks such as vases or plant holders or just as decorations, like what Jane did with her shadowbox.

Below the ads she saw an article from *Emergency Medicine News* Toxicology Rounds, with interesting information Jane hadn't mentioned: The pong pong tree is also referred to as the suicide tree! The seeds contain a white kernel that has been used for suicide in India for a long time. The article stated that they are bitter, but the bitterness can be hidden if they are mixed into a spicy dish.

She read: "The kernel of the pong-pong seed contains high concentrations of cardiac glycosides—cerberin, cerberoside, neriifolin—that have actions similar to digoxin. They inhibit the Na+-K+-ATPase pump, impairing the exchange of sodium and potassium across the myocardial cell membrane during cardiac repolarization. The result increases irritability of the atria and ventricles, decreases conduction through the AV node, and increases extracellular potassium."

From the case report she read: "All patients presented with vomiting as the initial symptom, which began three to 15 hours after ingestion. ... Five of the six patients developed bradycardia with pulse rates less than 40 beats per minute. Four of six had hyperkalemia."

Heart problems, vomiting, high potassium. It all fit. What if the seed thief used pong pong seeds to poison Pat? When Jane had told her someone stole some of her pong pong seeds, she apparently hadn't been aware that they were poisonous. Who else could have known that? Could the seeds be the brown woody substance in Pat's stomach? And would the medical examiner even know what to look for?

Pearl printed out the web page. She had to tell Jane what she had discovered. She grabbed her raincoat and pulled it on one sleeve at a time as she moved around the house. She opened the freezer, got a frozen raw chicken wing out, and threw it to Buckley to keep him distracted while she was gone. Then she snatched her purse, fumbled the keys out of it and rushed to the car with the printout from the Toxicology Rounds website.

Pearl sat silent in Jane's living room as Jane perused the paper Pearl had handed her after she pounded on and then burst through the front door. Jane couldn't understand everything she was reading, but she could understand the obvious: pong pong seeds are poisonous and people have used them to commit suicide.

Jane shook her head as she read. "That's interesting, but I don't understand all the medical stuff. What are you thinking? That Pat might have stolen the seeds and killed himself?" she finally asked Pearl.

Pearl put her hand to her forehead, then shook her head vigorously. "No, but I do think we've been on the wrong track. Suicide makes no sense. Pat was happy. He had you and he had just gotten an inheritance. But somebody had it out for him. I don't know if it was because of his inheritance—which is still missing, by the way—or some other reason. Everyone agrees that there were people who didn't like him."

"You mean you think someone poisoned him?" Jane's face turned ashen, as the obvious answer dawned on her.

"Yes, I do. Sheriff Dan came over yesterday to buy some milk and he told me they found a brown, woody substance in Pat's stomach contents. I know he vomited before he died because I saw it on the trail. That's one sign of pong pong poisoning that the page refers to. Remember how Joe said Pat's color wasn't good? Well, when I talked to Dave, he also told me Pat had an upset stomach, which was his excuse to have a celebratory scotch and soda. And the sheriff told me before that the medical examiner found high potassium in his blood—another effect of the seeds. Of, course we can't know if his heart rate was slow, but otherwise, it all fits together. So now we need to figure out who could have stolen your pong pong seeds. Do you know who came through your house for the Garden Club Tour? Maybe we could make a list."

"I hope this isn't another wild goose chase." Jane looked perplexed.

Pearl glared, irritated. "And what else do we have to do now that it's winter? We both cared about Pat, so let's get to the bottom of this. It won't hurt anything and it might help."

"You're right," Jane conceded. "As a matter of fact, I have a garden club meeting tomorrow. I could get the list of people on the tour then, along with a list of all the garden club members. Remember, though, they could also have learned about pong pong seeds through one of the catalogs. We don't know that the person who stole my seeds necessarily used them for murder. They would have had to be aware they were poisonous. I'm sure I'm not the only one who doesn't know every extraneous detail about the seeds she buys."

"How many people would you say attended the Garden Club Tour?" Pearl ignored Jane's point about not knowing details about seeds. *Why do people lack basic curiosity or desire for knowledge?* She picked up her tea and sipped at the hot liquid, burning her lip. She set it back down, gripped the teabag label, and bobbed it up and down to release the tea and cool the liquid.

"I'm not sure. I think maybe 20 people. I'm sure they have a list of all those who signed up for it."

Pearl absentmindedly chewed on the inside of her cheek, her brow furrowing. "Another thing we need to figure out is where the chicken came from."

Jane shifted in her chair. She appeared confused.

Pearl stared hard at her. "Oh, sorry. Dan also told me that they found partially digested chicken in Pat's stomach. Both the Pub and the Armadillo Café serve food and have specials, so we need to find out what each of them was serving. That might give us another clue as to who could have poisoned him.

"This information about the seeds changes everything." Pearl sat up straight and gesticulated. "If someone did poison Pat, they wouldn't have had to follow him like I originally thought; they just had to put poison in something he ate or drank and wait for him to die. Tell me when you get those lists. Then we can start ruling people out."

"Or in." Jane looked grim.

🏠

Westin showed up the next day. Buckley was glad to see him, as usual, but Pearl was a different story. *How would she approach him about his lie?* With her new theory about the pong pong seeds, she seriously doubted that he had the opportunity to poison and then rob Pat. The effect of the seeds wasn't instantaneous, after all. It would have taken hours, with him waiting for Pat to collapse. *Why did the thought that he might kill his friend ever cross her mind, anyway? Westin was so kind-hearted and had been friends with Pat for years. And how would he even have known about Pat's inheritance?*

"Hi, Pearl." Westin wore crisp new jeans, a navy blue hoodie, and shiny new leather lace-up boots. "I was just stopping by to tell you I'm going to Eastern Oregon with a friend for a few weeks. In case you needed help with anything right away.... What's wrong?" A flash of concern crossed his face.

Pearl tried to smile, but her face betrayed her. "Let's sit on the porch. I want to talk to you about something."

Westin looked apprehensive as he followed her to the porch and took a seat. Buckley jumped onto his lap, oblivious to what was happening.

"What's going on?" Westin let out a nervous laugh.

"Westin, I'll get right to the point. Why did you lie to me about when you got back to Middle Pass from the coast?"

Redness crept up Westin's neck until his face was ruddy. He ducked his head. Silence. He started to pet Buckley.

Pearl waited, not saying anything.

"I don't know. I don't like people knowing my schedule. I'm a private person. When you told me Pat was dead, I had already said I just got back that morning and I didn't want to admit that I hadn't been straight about seeing him two nights before."

"So now you admit you saw him the night he died?" Her eyes narrowed.

"Yes. But he was mostly fine then, other than the drinking. It wasn't actually a lie; it was a misunderstanding. I was just speaking in general about being back recently. And with the police involved, I didn't want to get in the middle of it. Maybe you didn't know, but I do have a record. It's just for pot, before it was legal, and once for some psychedelics. Nothing violent, but I haven't had good experiences with law enforcement. I was kind of relieved when I heard that the sheriff said he had been drunk and accidentally fallen on the way home."

"Are you sure he was fine? Tell me everything about that night," said Pearl earnestly. "I want to trust you, but you need to be honest with me."

"He was just leaving the Pub when I drove up. He was talking to a Hispanic guy and they exchanged something. I shouted at him and he came over to the van. He seemed a little tipsy, which was unusual. He told me he had just inherited a bunch of money and had celebrated with a drink. I could tell he felt kind of bad about drinking again after all this time. I guess I'm a terrible influence. He asked if I could give him a ride to the path. He planned to walk home from there. And he had borrowed money from me over the years, and I thought maybe I could get some of it back.

"We got to talking and I had a six-pack, so I offered him one. I had pulled off the road a ways and we hung out, talking and drinking. I told him I was low on funds and asked if he could pay back some or all of the money he owed me, and since he was lit up, he agreed pretty easily.

"I think he had two beers total. At some point I noticed he was sweating heavily and then he said he had a headache and his stomach hurt. The last thing he needed was another beer. I told him he should just go home and not drink any more. I offered to drive him, but he said he wanted to walk so he could get some fresh air. I guess I should have offered to walk him back to his house.

"I stayed there in my van for the night because it was off the road and concealed from the traffic. I didn't see him after he left. In the morning, I got up and went into town, not knowing that anything had happened to him. Then the next morning I decided to stop by and check in with the two of you. I had no idea he hadn't made it home that night."

Pearl had been listening intently. *If only Pat had accepted the ride.* "Do you know what time he left to walk home?" she asked.

"I think around 7:00 or 7:30."

Pearl raised her eyebrows and stared at Westin, "Did you know how much money he had when you met up? He didn't have any money when they found his body."

Westin cringed but said nothing.

"What about all the money you've had lately? You bought me lunch at the Armadillo and now you have new clothes. How much money did he repay you?"

140

He shook his head and didn't respond.

"Why aren't you answering me?" Pearl stared at him without dropping her gaze.

Westin looked hurt. "How can I prove I didn't do something? I'm just disappointed that you don't believe me. I'm sorry I didn't tell you the truth that day, but I'm doing it now. Like I said, I knew Pat had gotten an inheritance because he told me that night. He didn't tell me how much. For the past year he had been borrowing $100 here and there when he knew I was doing well. He seemed proud of being able to pay me back the $400 he owed me that night. With that and what you paid me for helping with the goat show, I bought some clothes. Am I supposed to live in rags? I guess I shouldn't have been generous and taken you out for lunch."

"No ... that's not what I meant," Pearl stammered. "I-I want to believe you. You've always been honest with me in the past. I just needed to ask these questions because our friend is dead, his inheritance money is gone, and you were probably the last one to see him. I'm sorry if I offended you, Westin. There is one more thing. What do you know about pong pong seeds?"

"What? Ping pong seeds?"

"Pong pong seeds. They're poisonous and someone stole some from Jane. We think that's what killed Pat."

Westin looked confused and scared. "I don't know anything about any seeds. Honestly, we just had a couple of beers together, he repaid me, and then he left. I don't know what else to tell you."

"All right. I believe you're telling me the truth. I'm sorry I had to talk to you about this, but I need to find out what happened."

Westin raised his voice. "Dang it, I said I *just* got back, not knowing at the time that Pat had died. Then I didn't correct your assumption because I was afraid this is what would happen. The police would think I killed him, and I had no way to prove a negative. It isn't fair. And now I'm suspected of robbing him, too?"

Pearl didn't react to his anger. "I can't promise the sheriff's office won't contact you, Westin. But it sounds like you have nothing to hide. Just tell them the truth if they do," she said calmly.

Westin's hands shook. "I have to get out of here for now. This is upsetting. I'll get ahold of you once I get back. I really hope you get to the bottom of this. Pat and I had our differences, but I would never hurt him. You have to know that."

Westin stood to leave, gave Buckley a final pet and set him down on the chair.

"I'm sorry about all this," mumbled Pearl.

"Me, too, said Westin, as he strode to his van, not looking back.

Chapter 15

Thank goodness for the goats and chores, thought Pearl, as she milked Jinx that evening. She was still stinging from the conversation with Westin. Her instincts told her he was being honest. And Buckley thought Westin was a good guy. *You're supposed to be able to tell whether someone is a good person based on how your dog acts around them.* The theory had always served Pearl well in the past, other than one time.

Jane had agreed to come right over as soon as she returned from the garden club meeting in the evening. Pearl hoped she had gotten the lists so they could go over them together. *They say the first 48 hours are the most important after a murder, and they were already past that.*

Pearl finished milking both goats. She strained the milk into a clean jar, put it into the barn fridge, and cleaned up. Then she emptied and refilled waters, refreshed the hay feeders, and sat in the main pen with the goats for a while. Being with the goats calmed her and helped her clear her mind. *Had she mishandled the conversation with Westin?*

After a half hour of goat meditation, Pearl gathered her milking equipment and returned to the house. Buckley didn't react when she came in. He had retrieved an old marrow bone and was working doggedly on it. Pearl cleaned her milking supplies and finished washing the dishes by the sink. She put the clean supplies and dishes in the drainer to dry.

She was at loose ends. She lay down on the comfy couch and her mind drifted back to her conversation with Dave. He didn't strike Pearl as someone who would go out of his way to cash Pat's check unless something was in it for him. Maybe it was just a ruse to get at the money. Still, Jane knew Dave better than Pearl did, and she didn't think $5,000 would have been motive enough to kill Pat. Still, Pearl thought Jane was more than a little naïve about hard drugs and what they can do to people. In her nursing experience, Pearl had seen plenty of people act irrational, out of character, or even worse from drug use.

If Dave was on that Garden Club Tour list, they had to go back and question him again. She hadn't thought to ask him if he got anything for cashing the check, other than a free drink from his own bar. *And why had he lied about being there all evening? If what Gina said was true, he would have had time to go get the rest of the money after Pat started down the path. Then again, how would he have known Pat was walking in the woods unless he had tailed him to Westin's van and waited?*

Her head swam with questions and Pearl drifted off. She was dreaming of the sheriff hauling a belligerent Dave off in handcuffs, when Buckley let out a shrill bark. She sat up straight. Buckley ran to the door yapping, and Pearl walked over to let Jane in.

Buckley jumped at Jane's leg. She reached down and held him to prevent a repeat performance. "Down, Buckley," she said firmly. He looked momentarily confused and sat down. Jane gave him two gentle pats on the head and walked across the room. Buckley got into his dog bed and lay down.

"Success?" Pearl brightened up.

"I got both lists," said Jane. "I just suffered through the most boring garden club meeting I have ever attended, not because of the subject matter, but because I just wanted to get the lists and come back here."

"Have you looked at them yet?"

"Not yet. I wanted to do it together. But I'm acquainted with most members; I'm less sure of who was on the Tour because we get people from all over the area. Luckily, we charge for the Garden Club Tour. The Tour and the annual spring plant sale are our main fundraisers for the year." She parked herself on the couch and placed the lists on the coffee table.

Pearl sat next to her and they each picked up a list.

"I didn't realize we had so many people on the Garden Club Tour that weekend. It looks like nearly 40! I remember some of the people who came through my garden, but this will confirm them," said Jane.

Pearl stood up, walked to her desk, and grabbed a tablet and pencil. "Let's make a list of who is a garden club member *and* was on the tour. Then we'll have a starting point to rule people out."

Jane compared the two lists while Pearl recorded each of the common people or couples. Unsurprisingly, all members of the garden club except two had attended the tour—Barbara DeWitt and Lorena Wilson.

"I think we're going about this wrong," said Jane. She shifted in her seat. "We need to identify people who might have had a motive." She set aside the garden club membership list and picked up the spreadsheet that listed people who had paid for the Tour.

Pearl moved closer and they reviewed the spreadsheet together. The names of the only two people on the list that stood out were Vern Davis and Dave Miller.

Pearl turned to Jane. "It looks like we were on the right track even before we considered that he was poisoned, when it comes to people who had a reason to kill him. Vern couldn't have known about the inheritance but if what Helen said is true, he may have had a grudge against Pat. Do you know why Lorena wasn't on the tour? Seems odd since she was so involved with the club."

Jane thought back. "I vaguely remember that Vern told me she had stayed home that day because she had a virus and didn't want to infect anyone else. Of course, I also remember that Dave was on the Tour. I did my best to ignore him, but he makes it hard. I don't know what I ever saw in that arrogant ass."

Pearl continued. "Dave had a motive, considering his financial trouble, and he knew about the inheritance before Pat even got the check. He was also jealous because you dumped him for Pat. The money may have been beside the point, or just a bonus.

"The only other two people we're aware of who knew Pat had a lot of money were Joe Martinez and Westin Denton. Neither of them was on the Tour, although I see

146

here that Joe's mother was. I can't imagine her stealing and, besides, at that point Pat didn't even have his inheritance yet. Joe only found out because he was in the Pub the night Dave cashed the check. So there goes his motive. I think we can easily rule Joe out. But then we knew that, after we met with him the other night, right?" Pearl bit her lip.

Jane nodded.

"By the way, I talked to Westin today. He's pretty pissed off right now. He admitted he knew of the inheritance because Pat had gone with him in the van to drink some beer. He claims Pat paid him $400 he owed him, but that was all. He said Pat must have had the rest of the money when he left to walk home, but he had no idea how much it was. He also told me Pat had been sweating heavily and complaining of a headache and stomachache when he started down the path. Which fits with pong pong poisoning."

Jane's eyes grew big. "That's a huge revelation we didn't have before. Do you believe everything he told you?"

Pearl gave a big sigh. "Actually, I do believe him about all of it. I don't know, even though he told that one lie, he seems like a basically truthful person. And, to be honest, I have a hard time believing he's a bad person because Buckley likes him so much. That probably sounds silly, but I trust my dog to tell me if someone is good or bad. And Westin hasn't ever seemed to care much about money, from what I can tell.

"I guess I should have asked Westin if Pat ate anything while he was in the van before I told him about the pong

pong seeds, though. He claimed not to know anything about them. Still, theoretically, I don't think the timing of Pat's death would rule him out as a poisoner." Pearl grudgingly added Westin Denton's name to the list.

She reviewed the spreadsheet one more time and started to hand it back to Jane. "Do you recognize the names of anyone else on the list who Pat knew? You probably have more of an idea about who he was friendly with than I did, since he kept so many things secret from me."

"Wait a minute." Pearl pulled the spreadsheet back and looked at it. "Ward Fowler," she said. "The guy who runs Ace Hardware. I'll add his name to the list, too. Zora said at the goat show that she knew about an altercation he and Pat had at one point. I had almost forgotten about that because I had to shut her and her gossip down before she ruined my day."

Jane looked pensive. "So, we have Vern Davis, Dave Miller, Westin Denton, and Ward Fowler on the list. I don't see any other names on the spreadsheet that stand out. Pat wasn't the most sociable guy. I think he preferred people one on one, rather than being in a group. He only went to the Pub once a week or so, I think, when they had the mashed potatoes and steak special. Not being a drinker, he was kind of an outsider with all the usual crowd."

"Did he ever mention any problem with Ward Fowler to you? We need to follow up on that connection at some point. Hey, let's go to the Pub right now and talk to Dave again. We can find out what they were serving that night and ask him again what he did after he cashed the check,"

Pearl pleaded with Jane. She felt energized at the progress they were making.

"There's no way I'm going down there with you, especially at night! I don't ever want to see or speak to Dave. Please just wait until morning. I don't want you going there by yourself. Maybe we should share this with the sheriff now." Jane wrung her hands.

"All right," said Pearl, a little too quickly. She realized she would never get Jane's assistance with talking to Dave. "Let's talk again in the morning after we've had time to think about it. I can go to Ace Hardware and maybe you could talk to Lorena tomorrow."

"I need to go to the café anyway. I haven't been there in over a week. But I also agree we need to sleep on it and maybe even come up with a clearer plan." Jane stood and stretched her arms over her head. "I'm exhausted. Between getting the garden ready for winter, the meeting, and now this, I just want to go home and go to sleep. How about you?"

Pearl nodded. "You're right. I'll see you in the morning."

She walked over to Jane and gave her a hug. Jane at first stiffened, but then she leaned into it. "Thanks for helping me find out the truth. It's the least we can do for Pat."

Jane nodded. She put on her coat and walked to the door. "Please think about calling Dan to report what we found out. The sheriff's office has the resources to do a proper investigation. After all, we may be dealing with a murderer."

Pearl rolled her eyes, then nodded reluctantly. But she had another idea.

"Good night, Jane."

Chapter 16

Pearl waited 15 minutes, then slipped into her raincoat. "You stay here, Buckley. I won't be long," she told the little dog, who stared at her. "On second thought, I'll get you a treat."

Pearl opened the freezer and took out a baggie of pasture-raised chicken feet and pried one from the others. They creeped her out, but the holistic vet had recommended them for dogs. She carried it to Buckley, who jumped up, wagged his tail, grabbed it, and retreated to his dog bed. *Spoiled brat.*

She scooped up her purse and keys and strode out the front door and through the drizzle to her car. Autumn was her least favorite time of the year. Wind, rain, falling leaves. Everything was dying. It made her want to stay in the house by the fire all day. Even snow was preferable. She drove down the long driveway and turned right onto the highway, then took the right on Crown Road, which led into Middle Pass.

Jane isn't used to the same kind of people I am, she thought. As a nurse in a hospital, Pearl had encountered drunks, drug addicts, people with severe mental illness, and more. She had been assaulted more than once. It was part of a hospital nurse's job description. She knew how to handle herself. *How dangerous could a small rural bar be?*

Traffic was light, but between the rain and the bright lights of the cars coming at her, she struggled to see the road. She was thankful for the short drive. The parking strips in front of the Pub were filled with motorcycles and big macho pickup trucks. She pulled into a spot a few stores down from the Pub, got out of the car and ran toward the entrance, holding her hood over her head with one hand and her purse in the other while she hopped over pools of water that had formed on the uneven sidewalk.

The odor of fish and chips hit her nostrils as she entered the Pub. All but a few stools at the bar were taken, as were the majority of tables and benches. A loud hum of conversations filled the air. Pearl scanned the establishment for Dave, but didn't see him anywhere. She noticed a different, older woman behind the bar. *Where was Gina?*

A yell pierced her thoughts, "Pearl! What are you doing here? Come and sit with us."

Her head turned in the direction of the voice, where Zora Vega, her husband, Tommy, and another couple sat at one of the long benches. Pearl felt a combination of relief and annoyance as she walked over.

"Oh, hi, Zora. I don't usually come out at night, but I needed to talk to Dave, the owner. Have you seen him?"

"I saw him earlier," Zora responded. She took a drink of her beer. "I think you've met my husband Tommy, and this is Joan and Tim Derryberry."

Pearl scanned the faces around the table as Zora spoke and nodded at each of them. "I'm Pearl. It's nice to meet you."

"Do you want anything to drink?" asked Tommy. "I was just about to go get another pitcher."

"I'd like a Bennett Winery pinot noir. It's their house wine. I had one the last time I came here and it was excellent." She opened her purse and fished out a ten-dollar bill. "This should cover it," she said to Tommy.

"Naw. This one's on me." He smiled. Pearl put the bill back in her purse as he stood and headed for the bar.

"What do you need to talk to Dave about?" asked Zora. "Do you still think he killed Pat?"

"I never said that!" snapped Pearl. *Leave it to Zora to misconstrue what she said at the feed store.*

"I actually want to talk to you about something you said at the goat show," Pearl folded her hands in her lap in an attempt to calm herself. "You had mentioned how Pat got into some kind of fight with Ward Fowler at the Ace Hardware store. What's the story?"

Zora's eyes lit up. She took a deep breath and began, "Oh, yeah. I heard that him and Pat had gotten into some kind of argument. I didn't hear any details of what it was about, just that Ward had complained about him coming in fixin' to make trouble."

Not much to go on, thought Pearl with annoyance. *It figures that Zora has no idea what she is talking about. She just likes to create chaos.*

"Who told you that?" she asked.

"I think it was my sister's husband, but I don't really remember. It was quite a while ago." Zora took the final gulp of her beer and looked at Pearl.

"Not really a reason to kill someone, is it?" she asked Zora. Zora just laughed.

Out of the corner of her eye, Pearl saw Dave come out from the back room and talk a to a rough-looking guy at the bar, gesturing wildly. She looked down at the wooden table, losing her courage for a minute. *Maybe this was a bad idea.*

As Tommy approached with the pitcher and her wine, Pearl recognized Dave's bald head and brawny body sauntering along behind Tommy. He was grinning and gladhanding people at the bar. Dave's eyes swept over the customers and locked on Pearl's. He increased his pace and came over to the table just as Tommy sat down.

"Hello, folks. I hope you're having a good evening. Pearl, what are you doing out tonight? We don't usually see you down here." He eyed the wine glass she had started to take a sip from. "I can't believe you came just for the house pinot noir." He rubbed his nose and sniffed.

"Hi, Dave. Where's Gina?" Pearl raised her eyebrows.

"I fired that little snitch! I don't need no employees talking out of turn."

"What do you mean?" Pearl tried to look innocent.

"You know very well what I mean, Pearl. You talked to her the other day when you were in here grilling me for doing a good deed." He rubbed his bald head.

"Speaking of that, I had a couple more questions for you. Can we talk in your office?" The Vegas and Derryberrys had stopped what they were doing and gaped in anticipation.

"Anything you've got to say you can say right here," he growled. "I have nothing to say that's a secret. I suppose this is about Pat again." He walked around and stood next to Pearl, rubbing his mustache with his thumb and one finger. His cologne was overpowering.

"Well, yes, kind of. Can you tell me what you were serving the night Pat died? And, did he eat here?"

"Friday night we had the mushroom burger special with fries or onion rings, like always. Why are you asking? You think he was poisoned or something?" he said, guffawing. Dave touched his Glock.

Pearl's tablemates tittered. "Do you have any chicken on the menu?" she asked.

"Look at the menu yourself!" Dave's neck began to flush.

"Okay. Did he eat here at all that night?" Pearl looked serious.

"No!" shouted Dave, looming over her. He leaned down toward Pearl, his reddened face inches from hers. She could smell the alcohol on his breath competing with the reek of cologne. "Why are you asking me these ridiculous questions? I thought the death had been ruled an accident. I do the man a favor and now I'm considered the bad guy? I don't appreciate you trying to make me look bad in my own business."

Pearl was taken aback. She hadn't expected such a strong reaction. But she pressed on. "One more thing ... were you here all evening after Pat left, like you said before? Or did you go somewhere else, like Gina told me?"

155

"I'm not gonna answer no more questions. This is bullshit! Just finish your wine and leave!" Dave stood up straight, turned, and stomped toward his office.

Pearl sat frozen for a minute, then looked around the Pub and observed surprised customers following Dave with their eyes as he stormed past. He stopped at the bar and said something to a large man sitting there—who looked over at Pearl's table—and the proceeded on to the back room. Pearl felt a shiver go down her spine.

"Wow, you really got to him," said Zora, her eyes big. "Not hard to do with someone who is flying high on coke, huh? Or is it steroids?" She snickered. "What was that all about, Pearl?" Her husband and friends stared at Pearl, saying nothing.

"Nothing," said Pearl, willing her face to blankness. "I probably shouldn't have come tonight." She took a drink of wine, thought better of finishing it, and set it back on the table. "Thanks for the drink, Tommy. It was good to see you, Zora, and to meet everyone. I better get out of here."

She dug through her purse and found her keys. With the keys in hand and her purse clutched under her arm, she headed for the front door. She looked straight ahead, feeling eyes on her as she passed.

As she tottered carefully around puddles to her car, Pearl heard the Pub door open and close. She didn't want to reduce her already slow progress by looking to see who was behind her, so she kept moving as heavy footsteps pounded the pavement, seeming to get closer. She could feel her heart thumping. She pushed the automatic unlock on her key fob and quickly got into her Subaru and locked the doors. She raised her eyes to see a large man getting into the big gray Dodge Ram truck two spaces down from her. *It's nothing; just someone else going home from the Pub.*

She started her car and backed out, then followed Crown Road toward the highway. She hadn't gotten to the first stop sign when she saw lights from the pickup truck behind her. She continued down the road and took a left onto the highway. The lights followed. She accelerated to 55 mph, the posted speed, and the lights came closer until the truck was almost on her bumper. Pearl increased her speed to 60 mph, then 65, but the truck continued to tailgate her.

Her heart pounded. *What if it was Dave or one of his drug buddies?* Her driveway was coming up. Pearl flipped on her left turn signal and began to slow the vehicle. She leaned forward to avoid being blinded by the bright lights that glared in her mirrors. The truck was inches from her bumper. She got to her driveway, slowed even more, and turned left. The truck accelerated and flew down the highway past her.

She parked in the driveway and sat in the dark, willing her pounding heart to slow down before going in the house. *It was probably nothing.*

Chapter 17

"I have to confess to having done a stupid thing," said Pearl to Jane the next morning as they sat in Jane's dining room drinking tea. Pearl had brought Buckley along, but this time he was clean and fluffy and rested quietly in her lap.

"What?" Jane raised her eyebrows.

"After you left last night, I drove to the Pub to ask Dave some more questions." She feared Jane's judgement. "I know I agreed not to go. I have no idea what came over me. After we narrowed it down to just three possibilities, I just felt a sense of urgency. Anyway, it didn't go well. He basically kicked me out and refused to answer some of my questions."

Jane's jaw dropped. "Pearl! Are you okay? He didn't touch you, did he?"

"No, he just screamed in my face. I'm okay. But I'm starting to agree with you that we need to involve law enforcement. When I was coming back last night a man in a pickup truck followed me from the Pub to my driveway. I was terrified. He tailgated me almost the whole way. I was sure he was after me." Pearl put her hand on her heart.

"We have to contact the sheriff anyway, to tell him about the stolen pong pong seeds and that we think they were used to poison Pat. And since Vern already had a violent reaction to Pat and Dave got so mad at me, I don't think it's such a good idea for us to push either of them."

Jane laughed and shook her head. "I could have told you that last night."

"Don't rub it in, Jane. We all make mistakes." Pearl flushed. She felt like a fool.

"Pearl, I thought about everything overnight, too." Jane looked serious. "As I was falling asleep, I realized I don't know exactly when those seeds were stolen. I only noticed them after the tour. But Westin helped me the day before the tour, so he had the opportunity as much as Dave and Vern did. How well do you know him? Did he have anything against Pat? And what about the missing money? Why don't you think that would be enough motive for a homeless guy like him?"

Pearl shook her head. She didn't want to consider the possibility. "He and Pat had their differences, but I just can't see it. Like I said, he has never seemed to care that much about money."

She paused, thinking. "But now that you mention it again, he has had more money than usual. ... And he took me out to lunch one day and he also had new clothes and boots. I just don't want to consider that.... Still, we can tell Dan everything and see what he comes up with.

"And I think one of us still needs to talk to Ward Fowler to find out there is anything to Zora's story. I forgot to mention, I saw her with her husband and friends at the Pub last night, too. When I asked for more details about what happened in Ace Hardware, she couldn't tell me anything of substance. Like that telephone game. Someone told her something they heard and then she repeated her version to me. But it wouldn't hurt for one of us to get a feel for what he thought about Pat and whether the conflict was so big that he would want to kill him."

Deputy Lila Deatherage and Sheriff Dan Springer, with Buckley on his lap, sat on the couch in Pearl's living room. Pearl sat in the rocking chair and Jane occupied the blue plaid overstuffed chair that faced them.

"Thanks for coming, Dan. We really appreciate it. Jane and I have uncovered some information we think is relevant to Pat's death. It's a lot, so I hope you guys can stay awhile. Where should we start?" she looked to Jane.

Jane held the wooden shadowbox with seeds in her lap. "I think we should start with the theft of the pong pong seeds," said Jane. Pearl nodded.

"Okay. You may be aware that I'm into gardening and my focus is exotic plants. Well, I ordered seven seeds—pong pong seeds—from Thailand. I tried to grow two of them, but only one survived. It turned into a unique tree with orange fruits. I still have to get someone to help me carry it into the greenhouse for the winter. It's in a pot out in the garden right now...

"Jane," said Pearl gently. "Focus."

Jane shot an annoyed look at Pearl, then continued, "Anyway, at some point during or before the Garden Club Tour, two seeds disappeared. They were in a bowl on my dining room table. I just considered the theft an annoyance until Pearl showed me what she had found."

Pearl jumped in. "I went on the internet and found out the pong pong tree is also called the suicide tree because it has been used in India and other Asian countries for suicide or homicide for many years. Here, I printed out some info from a website I found." She handed the pages to the sheriff. "It can cause cardiac arrest."

"You know how the medical examiner said he found an unidentified woody substance in Pat's stomach contents and he had high potassium? Well, the seeds would explain both. The effects are the same as digoxin poisoning. I'm really interested in the other autopsy results—if it ever gets done—to find out if the medical examiner thinks this could be the cause of death." Pearl's voice rose and she began to rock in her chair.

"In the page from the Philippine Medicinal Plants, there's a mention of a test called high performance thin layer chromatography that can detect the substance in blood. I know you took blood for toxicology, so this should also be looked for. I think you need to follow up on this, Dan. From what people who saw Pat that night told me, he had symptoms that fit. He had a headache and upset stomach, he was sweating—something made him sick."

Pearl leaned back in her chair and sat still. She and Jane locked eyes and fell silent, while the sheriff and deputy read the papers.

"Do you have any more of these seeds?" asked the sheriff.

"Yes, I do. The remaining three are right here in this shadowbox. I like to make these with different seeds, herbs, and flowers. It's kind of a secondary hobby to my gardening." Pearl bit her tongue to keep from trying to stop Jane's rambling.

Jane lifted the shadowbox she had brought over and handed it to the sheriff. "Based on what I read, they would have had to cut open the seeds and remove the white kernels to hide them in food."

The sheriff and deputy took some notes and perused the documents. The sheriff shook his head and took a deep breath. "Can we keep these?"

"Of course," said Pearl.

Deputy Deatherage set the shadowbox and the papers on the coffee table.

"What else do you have?" asked the sheriff.

"Jane got a list of all the garden club members as well as a list of people who attended the Tour. We figured the most likely suspects would have been on the tour, although it's possible another garden club member could have ordered seeds from a catalog, like Jane did. Then we considered who might have had a motive to harm Pat. That led us to three possible suspects: Dave Miller, Ward Fowler, and Vern Davis. Although I am not so sure about Ward. He owns the Middle Pass Ace Hardware store. He did attend the Garden Club Tour, but I'm not convinced he had either motive or opportunity. We only included him as a suspect because of something another goat person told me. It still needs to be checked out." Pearl started to rock again.

"Here are the lists. You can have them, too." Jane handed the paperwork to the sheriff.

"Why do you think Dave and Vern have motives?" The sheriff looked from Pearl to Jane.

"Well, while Dave cashed Pat's $5,000 inheritance check for him, the money Pat still had after paying a couple of debts disappeared between the Pub and where he was found. Dave knew about it days in advance, *and* they serve food at the Pub, so he easily could have poisoned Pat, then left to follow him on the path and steal his money. While he claimed he didn't leave the Pub that night, Gina, the bartender, told a different story. And got fired for doing so.

"However, for what it's worth, their special that night was mushroom burger and fries. Not chicken, but he could have had chicken at the café and then Dave could have put the seed in something else. They serve snack food at the Pub, right? I got a few more answers out of Dave last night, but when I started to ask him more questions, he got enraged, screamed in my face, and refused to answer. I have witnesses to our conversation; most of the customers heard him."

The sheriff shook his head in disbelief. "Pearl, I told you to be careful. What were you doing down there last night alone, anyway?"

Pearl felt her face flush. "I just got carried away. I think we're on to something and I thought I could get some more information and help find the killer. We called you this morning after we realized we couldn't do it ourselves." She chewed at the skin on her lower lip.

"Speak for yourself," huffed Jane. "I told Pearl I thought we should call you after we talked last night." Pearl glared at her.

"Moving on. I suppose you consider Vern Davis a suspect because he serves food? Is there any other reason? What would his motive have been?" The sheriff raised his eyebrows and stared at the two women.

"Vern and Pat didn't get along at all. You need to talk to Helen—I don't know her last name," said Pearl. "She's at the Armadillo Café most days; she usually sits with Larry and Shirley at the end of the counter. They're all locals and, in fact, maybe Larry and Shirley could confirm Helen's story. Anyway, when I was retracing Pat's last hours before he died, I found out he had eaten there. I didn't think to ask *what* he ate; I just asked about what had happened there that day.

"When I walked to the store afterwards, Helen rushed over to tell me about a verbal altercation Pat and Vern had had previously. Apparently, Vern got pretty worked up and threatened to kill him."

The sheriff and deputy both made notes. "So you don't know what the café was serving that day or what he ate?" asked the sheriff.

"No, like I said, it hadn't occurred to me at that point that *what* he ate might have been important. I was trying to find out about his mood and whether he had an alcoholic drink at the time. My working theory on his death at that point was that someone had followed him and hit him over the head." Pearl wrung her hands.

"I think this is enough to get us started," said the sheriff. "We'll follow up with the medical examiner and use this information and the lists to consider any leads. And we'll find out who Helen is and talk to her and anyone else who might have witnessed the incident between Vern and Pat. Can you think of anything else, Lila?" The sheriff gave his deputy an intense look.

"I think we have enough here to keep us busy," she said. She began to gather the paperwork and the shadowbox.

"There's something else you need to consider." Jane looked at Pearl and then at her lap. "Pearl doesn't think it was him—while I can't imagine it being Vern—but Westin Denton helped me with my plants the day before the Garden Club Tour and, to be honest, I can't say for sure if the seeds vanished that day or during the Tour. Things were so busy I didn't notice them missing until a day or two afterward."

Pearl looked at Dan. "Did you ever talk to him after I told you Joe Martinez saw Pat get into a navy blue van?" she asked.

"No, I didn't have an address for him and it didn't seem that important. We weren't investigating the death as a murder."

"Well, I talked to him," said Pearl. "He admitted he gave Pat a ride that night. He said they drank a couple of beers in his van and then Pat left, saying he wanted to walk so he could get some fresh air. Westin said Pat felt sick. He also said Pat had mentioned his inheritance—but not the actual amount—and even paid back $400 he had owed him, but he had nothing to do with the rest of the money missing.

"The thing is, if he stole the pong pong seeds, it's unlikely he would even have known they were poisonous. I don't think he even has access to the internet. And he wouldn't have had any knowledge of the inheritance at that point, or that Dave was going to cash the check. So he wouldn't have had a motive."

Jane looked skeptical. "I think you need to consider every possibility."

Pearl stiffened, then went on, "And what about the timing of the death, Dan? Has it been determined? You would have to take that into account…."

"Where is he now, Pearl?" The sheriff didn't respond to her question about the time of death. "I'd like to talk to him."

"He left to camp in Eastern Oregon with a friend. I'm not sure exactly where they were going or when he would be back. He wasn't too happy with me when he left because he thought I was accusing him of the murder or theft."

"Well, let's not start calling it a murder just yet. Our preliminary conclusion was that it was an accident. I don't want to get the community alarmed over nothing. Please don't say anything to anyone until we learn more." The sheriff gave her a stern look and Lila nodded in agreement.

Pearl rolled her eyes and glanced at Jane.

The sheriff looked unsympathetic. "When Westin gets back, have him give me a call. In the meantime, I hope you learned your lesson last night, Pearl. You need to step back and let us work with this information. We do appreciate what you've found so far, but your safety is more important. I hadn't planned to investigate any further, but what you've shared is compelling. We'll let you know what we find out, but it's going to take some time."

Chapter 18

The days crawled by, with the temperature dropping, winter coming on, and a lull in Pearl's investigation of Pat's death. Other than a short visit to Ace Hardware, under the pretext of purchasing a new pitchfork, Pearl had taken to heart the sheriff's admonition to stay out of things.

That visit had been a waste of time, other than her purchase of the five-tine manure fork Ward Fowler recommended. Despite Zora's story, Pearl found Ward a jovial man who claimed to like Pat. He shared stories of their good-natured arguments and mentioned Pat's intellect. Like Jane and Pearl, he found Pat to be a likeable curmudgeon.

Ward had also been unaware of Pat's death until Pearl told him. She asked where he had been the night Pat died. The ruddy-faced man just laughed and told her, "at home watching television with the wife, like always." Pearl was not inclined to question him beyond that; without any evidence, she realized it was just more rumormongering from Zora.

As they waited impatiently for an update from the sheriff, Pearl and Jane tried to keep themselves busy. Despite their different focuses—Pearl with goats and Jane with plants—both had a lot of work to do in between the October rain storms that were so common in Western

Oregon. Pearl had to get the barn mucked out and clean straw bedding put down one last time before winter arrived. Throughout the winter she only needed to add new straw to create deep bedding that would compost and keep the does warm.

The growing musky buck odor also alerted Pearl to another autumn chore—planning which doe to breed to which buck and getting them together—while keeping the other does and bucks away.

Jane had to get her exotics and other cold-sensitive plants moved to the greenhouse, mulch plants, dig bulbs, prune bushes and trees, and clean and oil her tools. She also had to plant spring bulbs and clean up the garden.

Their work went into limbo when the rains began several days earlier, with a vengeance. They each planned to do as much as they could once the weather broke. Both of them were accustomed to solitary work. By the same token, the two women missed the help they would have gotten from Pat and hoped Westin would come back once the rains stopped, so he could take some of the burden off them. Routine chores couldn't be avoided, but Pearl refused to do the backbreaking work of mucking composted hay and alfalfa off the barn floor. Jane could move the smaller plants but couldn't lift some of the potted plants—which had grown over the summer—onto a wagon to move them. Instead, each of them thought it better to stay out of the rain and focus on what she *could* do—and only do that.

Pearl sat in the living room next to the blazing wood stove while she worked on her breeding list and listened to the rain pound on the roof. Buckley lay in his dog bed, gnawing on a fresh marrow bone Pearl had given him to keep him occupied.

She read that a good buck to doe ratio was 1:5 and a good buck could even breed up to 50 does. She had two bucks for seven does. In order to avoid inbreeding, she had traded the buck she used the prior year for a different, unrelated one and had bought another one from a different herd. She had the minimum two necessary to keep each other company.

Now she would have to decide which doe to breed to which buck and figure out a way to get them into a secure space for breeding without the other buck barging in uninvited. She pulled out the notebook of ADGA paperwork, and reviewed her animals' pedigrees. Pearl felt a twinge of conscience about breeding her goats because she had long been opposed to dog and cat breeding and the overpopulation that continued to plague the world. She knew that mammals produce milk in response to demand, so she considered whether to avoid breeding some of her does and milk them for another year or two before re-breeding. She decided to take that approach.

She would continue to milk Jinx and Kea but would breed their two daughters for kids the following spring. The doelings from this year could wait another year before she bred them. *That makes things easier,* she thought. She would start by tracking their heats and mark the calendar for three weeks later. By then Westin should be back to help.

As Pearl sat in her chair, her mind drifted to new kids in the spring and soon she dozed off.

Next door, not wanting to be in the drenching rain with a wheelbarrow and shovel, distributing piles of compost and mulch on the gardens or digging up bulbs, Jane chose a warmer and more entertaining pursuit. She gathered the seed catalogs that had begun to come in the mail and began to peruse them, circle the plants she wanted to buy, and fantasize about her garden next year.

Comfy on the couch, she reached for the pile of catalogs on the end table, pulled out the one from Baker Creek Rare Seeds that had arrived earlier in the week. She began to leaf through it, envisioning the colorful flowers she would add to her garden for the next year. Jane pulled out her tablet of graph paper and began to pencil in the plant names in the areas where she wanted them.

An hour later, the shrill ring of the telephone caused Pearl to awaken with a start. She must have drifted off and her breeding plans had turned to dreams. It was Jane.

"Pearl!" Jane sounded excited. "You'll never guess who just called me. Lorena! She was hysterical and she told me the police had just arrested Vern. They closed the café for the day, but I told her I'd come down and talk to her. Do you want to come with me? I hope she doesn't mind, but with your nursing experience you are probably better at de-escalating people and helping them calm down."

"Yikes! Did she say any more? Of course I want to go with you. I've been wondering about the investigation, but didn't want to bug Dan." Pearl's heart pounded. She would have bet money that Dave was the culprit. After all, he knew about the money, he was in financial trouble, and he had the opportunity to sneak a pong pong seed or two into some food—even a snack. Not to mention that he wasn't in the Pub during the key time and lied about it.

"She was babbling and sounded hysterical, so I don't know what she was trying to say. Get ready and I'll be there to pick you up in a few minutes." Jane hung up abruptly.

When they arrived at the café, the parking lot was empty except for Vern and Lorena's car—a rare sight on a Thursday. The parking lot was usually at least half full. Jane and Pearl looked at each other.

As Pearl and Jane got out of the car and walked toward the café, they saw movement behind the light-colored curtains. Jane, with Pearl behind her, knocked on the door. Through the window on the door, they had a view of Lorena behind the counter near the kitchen. She lifted her head and they could see that her eyes were puffy and tears streamed down her face.

"Lorena, what's going on?" yelled Jane. "Is there anything we can do to help? Let us in."

Lorena shook her head, hesitated for a minute, and then made her way to the door. They stood back as she unlocked the door and opened it.

Jane and Pearl came in the door and Lorena shut and locked it behind them. Then she half-moaned, half-shrieked, "They've arrested Vern!"

She continued, "A bunch of deputies came earlier and searched the whole place while we were getting ready for the breakfast rush. They made us sit out in the dining area while they did it. We put up the closed sign so no one else came in. I was mortified to see some of the regulars park and mill around outside. This is going to ruin us!" she said with bitterness.

"What was it about?" asked Jane. She gave a side-eye to Pearl.

"We found out they were searching our house at the same time. After they finished the search here, they had us wait. Then a call came that they had found some evidence at the house. They said it gave them probable cause to arrest Vern for Pat's murder. They brought up his record from back in Texas. But that happened years ago. He was young, he served his time, and he changed. He would never hurt anyone. Vern isn't that kind of man."

"What was his record for?" asked Pearl.

"Assault. But it was a long time ago. He always gets targeted because he's black. I am so sick of it." Lorena started to cry again. "It's all my fault," she sobbed.

"What do you mean?" Jane put her arm around Lorena.

"They asked me who does the cooking and I said Vern does," she moaned.

"Well, he does, doesn't he?" asked Pearl.

"Yes, but … they're saying he poisoned Pat. I know he didn't do it."

"Poisoned? Do you know for a fact that he didn't do it?" asked Pearl.

Lorena pulled away from Jane and glared at Pearl with hatred in her eyes. "Of course I'm sure! We moved up here for our dream of running this café and to get out of Texas. But it's never good enough. No matter where we go, my husband has to face prejudice because he's black! We both have to face it because we're an interracial couple. I'm so sick of it. We worked hard to make this place a success but then people like Pat have to come in and try to tear it all down.

"Vern would never hurt a fly! He tolerates so much crap and stays calm through it all, but Pat just kept pushing and pushing. I couldn't stand to see my Vern react like that. He's tried so hard. I thought there was supposed to be less racism in Oregon than in Texas.

"I can't stand the thought of him sitting in a jail cell. He was crying when he left here in handcuffs. Crying! What am I going to do? I *know* he's innocent!"

"Are you sure?" asked Pearl in a soothing voice. "Sometimes people can only take so much and they snap." She looked out the window at traffic crawling by and noticed on the windowsill a half-dead plant between a couple of other thriving plants that Lorena had proudly displayed there. *Where had she seen a plant like that before?*

Then it hit Pearl. The dying plant was a pong pong tree. That *was* what had killed Pat, and Lorena did it. That was why she was so sure that Vern hadn't.

Lorena fell to her knees, sobbing. "He's my husband! I know he wouldn't hurt anyone. He doesn't even know what a pong pong seed is."

There it was. Lorena had just inadvertently confessed that *she* knew what a pong pong seed was. Pearl had assumed, just like the sheriff, that Vern was the killer because he was so angry with Pat, without even considering that Lorena might have done it. That made so much more sense; after all, she was the gardener in the family and it's common knowledge that women are more likely to kill with poison than men are.

"Lorena, *you* know what a pong pong seed is, don't you? And you know that Vern didn't put pong pong seeds in Pat's food because you did it, didn't you?" asked Pearl as gently as possible.

Then it all came pouring out. "I just couldn't take Pat's abuse anymore! I never thought it would kill him. I can't stand the idea of Vern being locked in jail for something I did! I'm so sorry." Lorena slumped in shock. She opened and closed her mouth like a fish out of water.

Jane and Pearl stared at each other, mouths open in surprise. Lorena had just confessed.

"Look at that dying plant, Jane. It's a pong pong bush, looking as unhealthy as the one at your house," Pearl said in almost a whisper, pointing to the plant in the window.

Jane looked toward the window, pursed her lips and nodded in recognition.

"Where did you get the pong pong seeds, Lorena?" asked Jane.

Lorena silently sobbed, not responding.

Jane and Pearl looked at each, waiting for a response. Finally Lorena started to speak again. "That day we were folding brochures, you showed me your tree and I saw the seeds on the table. I had decided we should grow some, too. When I searched online to order them, I learned that they were poisonous and the tree is even called a suicide tree. But I wanted it for the orange fruits and small size, not to poison anyone. I had even planted the one in that pot in the window to see if it would grow.

"Then one day Pat got carried away with his insults to Vern. It was one of the few times that I'd seen Vern lose his temper. Later, I thought about those pong pong seeds. I brought one down to the café and stashed it in the kitchen, only half planning to use it. But nothing had changed with Pat. Vern was cooking that day—like usual—and on an impulse, before I served the chicken curry to Pat, I crushed half a seed and put it in his meal. Vern had no idea what I had done. He doesn't pay all that much attention to the plants and seeds I order.

"I figured just a half seed in the curry, Pat wouldn't be able to taste it, and if he got sick he would stay away and maybe he wouldn't come down here to eat anymore at all. That would solve our problem and we could carry on with our dream. But then Pat died. I hope it wasn't the pong pong seed that killed him." Lorena let out a long wail.

"Here, Lorena. Sit down. You're upset," said Jane. She put an arm around Lorena's shoulder and led her to a chair. "We're going to have to call the sheriff. I'm sorry. You can tell him the whole story."

Lorena gave a slight nod and continued to sob, "I know. I don't want to go to jail, but my poor, poor Vern didn't deserve this. I can't believe this happened."

Pearl walked behind the counter, took the phone off the hook, and dialed the sheriff's office.

Chapter 19

At the first bark from Buckley, Pearl peeked out the window. She saw the sheriff get out of his car with a bouquet of mixed flowers and an empty milk jar. She watched him move toward the house. He dodged raindrops and stepped onto the porch. She opened the door and Buckley raced out to greet his friend.

Once in, he handed the flowers to Pearl, placed the clean jar on the table, and lifted the wriggling Pomeranian who had been jumping at his legs in excitement.

"The flowers are a thank you for your poking around—with positive results this time. I still don't know how you got Lorena to confess." He chuckled, shaking his head. "I told you I would give you an update once we got things resolved."

"Oh, it all would have come out at some point anyway," Pearl looked bashful. "Would you mind if I call Jane so she can hear this, too? After all, I doubt Lorena would even have let me in the café if Jane hadn't been there. They're friends from the garden club. I don't think Lorena has many friends."

"Sure," said the sheriff. "I can wait. How about a glass of that delicious goat milk while we wait?"

Pearl found a vase for the flowers and filled it with water. She set the vase on the table and arranged the flowers to her satisfaction. She poured Dan a glass of goat milk and started the coffee for herself and Jane. It had just finished perking and Pearl was getting the cups out when Jane knocked at the door, then let herself in.

"Thanks for calling me, Pearl. I'm curious about exactly what happened after you took Lorena to the station." She took off her coat, hung it on the back of a dining room chair and took a seat.

Pearl carried a small cream pitcher filled with goat milk and a sugar bowl to the table. She made another trip from kitchen to table, bringing the steaming mugs of coffee and spoons for each of them. They sat around the table as Sheriff Dan began his story.

"I'd like to hear how you got Lorena to confess, but first I'll tell you how we arrived at Vern as the culprit.

"After Lila and I met with you and Jane, we took the pong pong seeds and literature on them to the medical examiner and explained that one of them may have been used to poison Pat. Oh, I have your shadowbox in the car, Jane. It's one seed short. We had to use it in our comparisons.

"After analysis and completing the autopsy, the medical examiner came to the conclusion that cardiac glycoside poisoning caused by ingestion of a pong pong seed led to Pat's fall, but the cause of death was a skull fracture that caused a brain hemorrhage. Apparently Lorena was telling the truth when she said she only poisoned the chicken curry with half a seed—a nonlethal dose.

"In the meantime, we were looking for Westin Denton. We still hadn't been able to find him. We also wanted to interview Dave Miller and Vern Davis again.

"You were right about Dave being touchy, Pearl, although he isn't quite as threatening to a law enforcement officer as to women, apparently." He laughed. "He declined a search of his business, and we couldn't match the Pub menu for that day with what was found in Pat's stomach contents—chicken—so we decided not to move further on Dave until we had investigated Vern a little more."

Jane snorted. "He was probably afraid you'd find drugs there. Everyone knows he has a coke problem."

"We interviewed both Vern and Lorena that morning. I personally talked to Vern and my deputy, Lila, interviewed Lorena. They both said that Vern had attended the Garden Club Tour and are members of the club itself. Lorena had a virus that day, so she stayed home. Vern acted nervous but, according to Lila, Lorena appeared calm throughout the interview. We didn't ask them about the seeds at that point, because we didn't want to give too much away. Then we asked them about how the work in the café is divided up and whether anyone else works there. They both agreed that Vern always does the cooking, that the special of the day had been chicken curry, and that Pat had ordered it. That matched with what we found in Pat's stomach contents. They also said they were the only ones working that day.

"I had already interviewed Helen Gunderson, who confirmed her story about a verbal altercation between

Vern and Pat, so we asked each of them about that. Vern admitted that he had lost his cool with Pat one day because Pat insulted Lorena. He claimed he could take the underlying racism and insults to himself, but you'd better not go after his wife. He claimed it was just a one-time thing and he had gotten over it, and, yes, he did threaten to kill him, but that's just something people say when they're mad.

"According to Deputy Deatherage, Lorena said, 'No, Vern never loses his cool.' She said everyone knows Helen is a gossip and you have to take what she says with a grain of salt. She denied that Vern had threatened Pat at all."

"It's certainly true that Helen is a gossip," said Jane. "Did you talk to others who were in the café at that time? Although, I guess if Vern admitted to making the threat, it must be true."

"Yes, prior to this we did interview other witnesses that Helen referred us to and they confirmed her story.

"When we asked if we could search the café, they both agreed to it. Based on what we had learned to that point, we had probable cause to get a search warrant for their home, as well. So while we searched the café, one of my deputies met with the judge to sign off on a search warrant for their home.

"We didn't tell Vern and Lorena we were searching their home, just that we wanted them to wait. We took our time searching the café. We found nothing of evidentiary value at the café. We did find some evidence at the house that showed a link between Vern and pong pong seeds. We found a receipt from an online seller for five pong pong seeds. Three seeds were found in their potting shed. So, interestingly, they weren't the seeds stolen from you, Jane. Once we got the word that that evidence had been located at the house, we arrested Vern.

"Besides the evidence linking him to the crime and the ongoing animosity between him and Pat, we had learned in the meantime that he served time in prison down in Texas years ago for almost killing another man. Both Vern and Lorena insisted that Vern was innocent and wouldn't hurt anyone, but we had probable cause to arrest him. It was pretty dramatic. We had to empty the parking lot of would-be customers, who were putting my deputies at risk. It's been a long time since I've seen so many angry people." The sheriff shook his head and chuckled, remembering.

"It seemed pretty cut and dry, so I was surprised to get your call when we were booking Vern. When you said Lorena had confessed, at first I thought she was just trying to confuse the situation or take the blame so she could get him out of jail. Well, she did get him out. After we interviewed them each separately for a second time, we believed that Vern knew nothing about what Lorena had done, so we released him and arrested her.

"Apparently, Lorena bought the seeds, but the credit card is in Vern's name, so it had appeared that he ordered them."

"What's she being charged with?" asked Jane.

"We initially charged her with first degree murder, although that is likely to change. It's for the DA to decide.

According to her confession, she didn't think a half seed would kill Pat. She claims she just wanted to make him sick so he would stop coming to the café. Not a real bright plan. It could easily have backfired if he had survived. And, if true, that wouldn't get her off the hook. The charge in Oregon for poisoning is up to life in prison, regardless of whether she intended to injure or kill him.

"This is what we believe happened: Lorena put a half a crushed pong pong seed in Pat's chicken curry, which he ate between 3:30 and 4:00. After he left the café around 4:45, he went to the Pub to have Dave Miller cash his inheritance check. They had a drink and he left the Pub between 5:30 and 6:00. He stopped to talk to Joe Martinez and pay back the $200 he owed him.

"As he was leaving the parking lot—according to what he told you, Pearl—Westin Denton drove up and Pat got into Denton's van with him. They drove partway home and then pulled off the road in a place Denton often sleeps in his van. They drank a few beers and then Pat went home, complaining that he felt sick. The medical examiner thinks he died around 8:30 or 9:00 that night.

"What we haven't figured out is why Pat's body was facing north when he fell. It would mean he was heading toward town, not toward Pearl's property, like Denton told you. He also didn't have any money when he was found, so we still need to follow up on what happened to the rest of the proceeds from Pat's inheritance check.

"You aren't going to like this, Pearl, but we're still looking at Westin Denton—if we can ever find him. He admitted to being the last one to see Pat alive. He also admitted to knowing that Pat had money from his inheritance. And he knew Pat wasn't feeling well. So who's to say he wasn't with Pat on that path and when Pat collapsed, he took the money and left him there?"

Pearl shook her head. "I don't believe that for a minute, but I understand why you might think that. You don't know him. One thing you missed in your chronology was that Pat repaid Westin the $400 he owed him. Not that it means he's innocent, but he had no reason to tell me that. I still believe he's innocent, even if we can't account for the rest of the money. I'm perplexed by the whole thing."

"Now, ladies, tell me: how did you get Lorena to confess?"

Jane started. "Lorena called me, hysterical, to say that Vern had been arrested. I knew that Pearl would be an asset with her nursing background, because the woman was out of her mind. Honestly, I only went over there as a friend to calm her down and offer some emotional support." She looked to Pearl, who continued from there.

"When we got there, Lorena was frantic but somewhat incoherent. She just kept saying she knew Vern didn't do it, but she didn't say why. I noticed a half-dead pong pong plant—evidence that your office obviously missed—about the time that Lorena let it slip, without any prompting, that Vern wouldn't even know what a pong pong seed is. That told me that *she* knew what a pong pong seed is. I realized that she knew more than she had been saying and, after some gentle coaxing, she finally broke down and confessed to having put half a pong pong seed in Pat's chicken curry."

"I doubt she would have confessed if Vern hadn't been arrested. She's very protective of him," Jane added somberly.

The sheriff finished his milk and stood up. "Well, this has been quite a case. I wanted to say again how much I appreciate the help we got from you two. Without your suspicions, Pearl, Pat's death would have been recorded as an accident and Lorena would have gotten away with murder or manslaughter.

"And Pearl, please let me know when you hear from Westin Denton again. We still have the issue of the money to follow up."

Chapter 20

After more than a week of pouring rain and howling winds that knocked most of the colorful autumn leaves from the branches, the sun reappeared. The creek was running strong and Pearl could hear it from the bedroom window she had opened for fresh air.

Jane had stopped by to give her an update on Vern and Lorena. She had talked to Vern at the café. He told her that he was selling it to make money for Lorena's legal fees. He was standing by her, despite her bad judgment. They hoped that because Lorena had no prior record and hadn't intended to kill Pat, the court would give her a lighter sentence. He said that unless she had to serve a lengthy sentence in Oregon or get probation that required her to stay in the area, they would move right back to Texas — which they had decided wasn't as bad as they originally believed.

With the sun, Pearl's motivation returned. For the first time in weeks, the goats would get to go on a hike, and she would get started cleaning the barn. But first, she would get the shed ready for Westin to move into if he wanted to stay. She still had not heard from him and the sheriff hadn't called to tell her he had seen him, either. But she was hopeful. *Maybe finishing the shed cleanup and putting on the fresh sheets would be the good juju needed to make things work out.*

Pearl carried the clean sheets, blanket, towel, and a damp rag out to the shed, then made another trip with the mop and soapy water-filled mop bucket as Buckley followed at her heels with his half-chewed marrow bone in his teeth. She opened the shed door and looked around. It appeared empty but cleaner, and the perspiration and human smell were only faint. She opened the window to air it out the remaining odor while she completed the finishing touches.

Before she could put the sheets on, Buckley jumped onto the bed with his bone, leaving faint damp tracks. "Buckley, you crazy furball! Get off that bed right now!" He remained there looking cute until she approached him and started to sweep him off the bed. He leaped down and stared at her defiantly.

Oh, well, the mattress probably needs to be flipped anyway. I doubt Pat ever did. She picked up the damp rag and swiped the dog tracks in an attempt to get the soil off. After two tries, she gave up and put the rag down. She lifted the bottom right corner of the mattress, rotated it and pushed it upward from the floor. She saw some papers flutter to the ground and another stack left on the floor. Pat's inheritance money!

Pearl retrieved all the bills that were scattered on the floor, then lifted the mattress corner again, picked up the remaining currency, and put all the bills in a neat pile. She realized that they were all $100s. Pearl picked them up and began to count: 1-2-3 … 43. $4,300. *It had to be what was left of Pat's inheritance. But how did it get here?*

Pearl put the stack of money on top of the table and finished flipping the mattress. Then she re-made the bed with clean sheets and blanket. She hung the fresh towel on the bar Pat had installed next to the microwave, and she mopped the floor, moving furniture as she went. All the while, her thoughts raced.

She felt vindicated. She *knew* Westin wouldn't have robbed or stolen from Pat. Especially when Pat was down and out—dying, actually. She had to call Jane to tell her she had been wrong with her hunch, and the sheriff to tell him to leave Westin alone.

Pearl took one last look around, picked up the stack of $100 bills and left the shed, with Buckley at her heels carrying his precious bone. They got as far as the porch when Westin's blue van clattered up toward the house. Pearl waved at him and continued into the house. When she got to her desk, she opened the middle drawer, pulled out a large rubber band and wrapped it around the stack of bills. She placed it in the drawer for safekeeping until she could turn it over to the sheriff with the $175 and change she had found earlier. Then she turned and walked back to the door just in time to meet Westin as he came in with a squirming Buckley under his arm.

"Your timing is perfect," said Pearl. "The rains just stopped so now we can get some work done. So much has happened since you left, so why don't you come in for a cup of ginger tea and I'll tell you all about it. And I have some great news!"

Pearl and Westin sat at the dining room table and drank their tea while she filled him in on the whole saga. "Finding the money also might explain why Pat was going north on the path. Maybe he had come home and put the money under his mattress and then for some reason—possibly because he knew he needed help and I wasn't home—he started back to your van or town. But he collapsed before he could make it. Sadly, we'll never know for sure what he was thinking."

"That would make sense," said Westin sadly.

"You're not still mad at me, are you? You know, I never believed you could have done anything to Pat. After all, look how Buckley reacts to you. That dog wouldn't be friendly to a killer or a thief. He has a second sense." She looked down at the Pomeranian and let out a little laugh.

Buckley wagged his tail in response to his name.

Westin laughed, too. "No, I'm not mad. Deep down I knew you were just looking out for Pat and you had to be suspicious of everyone. But I hope you've called off the dogs, so to speak. Apparently the sheriff put out an APB for me and my van. When I was coming down I-5, I got pulled over and given an escort to the sheriff's office in Eugene. I would have gotten here earlier if I hadn't had to spend two hours being grilled about my whereabouts and activities the night Pat was killed. They even searched me and my van — looking for money, I guess. Of course they didn't find anything so they had to let me go. I gave them your address as a contact; I hope you don't mind. I managed to stay cool through the whole ordeal, though. Something about camping in Eastern Oregon just calms a person down. Such wide, open spaces and no one to bother you.

"In a way, it's too bad I didn't take the money," added Westin, wistful. "I mean not that I would want to steal from Pat, but if he has no relatives, it will all revert to the state. So no one will benefit."

Pearl laughed and shook her head. "I know, but you gotta do what's right. Integrity is one thing that can't be taken away from you. And things do work out; right? Besides, he must have some relatives, since he just got that inheritance from his uncle. I hope I can just turn it over to the attorney who handled the inheritance. It's a shame Pat never got to enjoy the money. As soon as we're done here, I'll call the sheriff to tell him about the money, so he'll leave you alone."

"Thanks. You've been a good friend, Pearl." Westin touched her arm.

"What are your plans now? I know you've been living in your van the last couple of years, so I wondered whether you'd be interested in staying here for the winter — or even longer if it works out. I just got the shed cleaned and ready for you to move in, if you do."

Westin's eyes lit up. "Wow. That's generous. I hadn't even thought about it."

"Why don't you think about it and let me know. I think it would be good for both of us. And Jane. You can help her, too. I can give you a stable place to live and you'll have more than enough paying work."

"I don't have to wait and think about it. I've thought about my life a lot over the last two weeks and I'd like a place to stay over the winter. And maybe even longer. I love the goats and Buckley—and you—and Jane," Westin chuckled. "It will give me a chance to figure out where I want to go with my life next."

"It's a deal, then," said Pearl. "So when do you want to start mucking the barn?"

They laughed.

Also by Cheryl K. Smith

Raising Goats for Dummies
Goat Health Care
Goat Midwifery
Raising Goats: Some Essentials (e-book)
Best of Ruminations Goat Milk and Cheese Recipes